DEATH IN MAGNERSTOWN

A cozy murder mystery set in Ireland

ANNE CROSSE

THE
BOOK
FOLKS

Paperback published by The Book Folks

London, 2018

ISBN 978-1-7310-7562-8

www.thebookfolks.com

In memory of my parents, Patrick and Margaret.

CHAPTER 1

Toby Jackson struggled out of bed with the thought that he was getting too old for this going to work lark. On the other hand he was luckier than most, he consoled himself. He was his own boss so to speak, in that he had no one to answer to. That was the advantage of being caretaker of the courthouse and the graveyard.

For the past twenty years he'd been in that position, and in five years' time he'd be retirement age. The pension would be enough to live on seeing as he had only himself to worry about; and if he continued the way he was living at the moment, there'd be no worries. A few pints every night in Dunworth's Pub saved him a fortune in fuel, when you weren't at home there was no need to heat an empty house. He ate his lunch at the pub every day. You wouldn't cook a dinner at home for the few euros they charged. With his nourishment catered for, there wasn't much else he needed. He wasn't one for style; what was the point of having several sets of clothing when you could only wear one lot at a time?

You didn't need a degree to do Toby's job. The cemetery gates had to be opened every morning at eleven and closed at six in the evening. The courthouse opened for business on the first Tuesday of every month at ten o'clock, and all he had to do on the day was hang around and look busy until the last case was heard. The rest of the month in the courthouse was easy, a bit of painting here and there, some dusting and sweeping around the place and anything else that might crop up. Yes indeed, there were several advantages to the whole setup. One such perk was he could slip away to Roy's Betting Office, conveniently situated just two streets away. He liked to put a few euro on a horse. If you're not in, you can't win – so the old adage went.

This morning, however, Toby was feeling a bit more hungover than usual, and the fault lay solely with an anonymous donor who had left the money for three whiskeys with the barman. This combination with his usual four pints of stout had taken its toll, but they had tasted so good at the time – especially when he was getting them for nothing. The part in the pub he remembered, but getting home was a complete blank. He wouldn't be so stupid in the future. It wasn't safe getting into a state like that. Anything could have happened to him, like walking out under a car for instance.

The kettle whistled – a mug of tea and a cigarette and he'd be as right as rain, but as soon as he had the thought, panic set in. He did have cigarettes, didn't he?

He needn't have worried. There were three unopened packets in his overcoat pocket. Starting the day without a cigarette was like tea without milk to Toby.

He gave the thumbs up to the absent benefactor who'd been more than generous not only with the whiskeys but with the smokes as well. These little payments usually resulted from favours he'd be asked to do in the graveyard. Things like the cleaning up of a grave, cutting grass, or removing moss off a headstone. The requesters were usually relatives of the interred who couldn't do the job themselves. Gladly they'd slip him a few euro or stand him a few pints in the pub. Last night's payment in kind came from yet another satisfied customer, but he couldn't for the life of him remember who it might be. True he had done a few favours in the last few weeks but he thought he'd been looked after for those.

It was nice of the latest donor not to identify themselves though, he liked that. There were the odd few people who made a big deal out of making their little payment in kind. They almost expected you to kiss their feet by way of gratitude for your reward.

The sound of a van pulling up outside broke in on his thoughts. Toby pressed his face up against the net curtain so he could see out. The curtain which had originally been white, had now taken on a brown hue on account of all the cigarette smoke wafting onto it. Nicotine was terrible for staining things. He shuddered to think what his lungs must be like.

He read the lettering on the van, 'Price Right Kitchens'. The new people across the road were spending a lot of money on that house. He still couldn't understand why they'd moved into the avenue at all. Geriatric Avenue was the nickname given to the area, simply because the large majority of residents were old and grey.

The new couple were in their early thirties. They had only the one child, a son aged eleven, and he was a bold one. He was forever kicking that ball of his, and sometimes it landed in Toby's garden. Not that there were any precious blooms to protect in Toby's little patch. The little brat would scale the gate to retrieve the ball, the cheeky so-and-so. Toby didn't know the lad's name, and he didn't want to know it either.

It was rumoured that the newcomers paid one hundred and forty thousand notes for the house. Pure madness considering his own mother and father bought this place, happily now his, for two and a half thousand pounds from the corporation. Granted, that was considered a lot of money all those years ago, but a right bargain judging by today's prices.

After lashing out a fortune the people across the road were still spending money to put the place right. Toby was well aware that even the cheapest kitchen cupboards could set you back five grand. Price Right Kitchens indeed, Price Wrong would probably be more apt. On that note Toby gave up the curtain twitching and headed to the hall to get his coat.

Toby opened his front door just as another van was pulling up across the road. It was the O'Donnell Brothers who owned the electrical shop on the main street. They had a reputation for not being cheap, but their excuse was that they prided themselves on stocking only the best products. The new family was going the whole hog with a cooker, washing machine and dishwasher he supposed. His poor mother managed with a black range for years, it was the only thing he changed after she died. He upgraded to a new gas cooker, and to be perfectly truthful, he only did it because he couldn't work the range. The upgrade was a bit of a waste of money looking back on it now. All he ever did was boil the kettle, and slap a bit of toast under the grill.

You could get all the food you wanted in Dunworth's Pub, even a fine breakfast of rashers, sausages and puddings served to you with toast and a pot of tea for only six euro. If you felt inclined to slave over a hot stove at home, you'd be forking out much more for the ingredients and the price of the gas on top of it.

The walk to the courthouse from Toby's house only took a few minutes, which was another big advantage. He didn't need a car to get to work, so there was another expense he'd been spared.

As Toby approached the courthouse, he was surprised to see the usual suspects with their solicitors already waiting in the yard.

"You're late, Toby, my good man," Mr Carter Jones junior said.

Toby fumbled in his inside pocket for his watch. He'd kept it there since the strap broke a few weeks back. He'd kept meaning to go to the watch repair woman, but he hadn't got round to it.

Mr Carter Jones junior pointed to his watch. "It is ten thirty," he said.

Toby cursed him under his breath.

The clock at home must have been slow, Toby realized. It always did that when the battery started to run down. "More expense," Toby muttered as he turned his key in the lock and flung open the courtroom door.

Toby gave up watching television when his set packed up, and he came up with the excuse he wasn't missing much. All that violence, blood and gore on the box used to send a shiver down his spine.

His mouth dropped open at the sight in front of him.

A figure was sitting on the judge's bench, and it was like somebody had thrown a bucket of red paint over it. Only it wasn't paint at all, it was blood.

The person was clearly dead, because no one could have lost that much blood and survived.

"Jesus Christ," Toby croaked.

Carter Jones took charge of the situation. Gently he pushed Toby to one side, closed the door then faced the startled onlookers. "Everyone listen up," he ordered. "I want you all to go home immediately. Court is cancelled for today."

Toby's legs felt like jelly, he needed to sit down before he fainted. He made his way to the low wall and threw himself down. A quick cigarette and he'd be as right as rain, he reasoned.

Carter Jones took out his mobile phone and started pressing buttons.

Toby drew the smoke down into his lungs. It was going to be a long day. A very long day.

CHAPTER 2

'Welcome to Magnerstown' the sign said. Maggie smiled wryly as she reached out to the passenger seat and patted the keys to her new home.

A cottage on a quarter acre of land meant she'd get plenty of fresh air and exercise keeping the garden and lawns up to scratch.

The small business that came with it had apparently been the local newspaper quarters. *The Crier*, it was called and was defunct since the death of the editor. The printing press and everything needed to churn out the local rag was still intact she'd been told.

Maggie thought she might try her hand at her own business: be her own boss, a flower shop perhaps. But there was no rush, she could take it easy for a while thanks to the large amount of money she made on the sale of the apartment. Even after paying for her new abode she still had plenty of cash left, and that was a real bonus. A bookshop could be another option.

Maggie laughed at the way her train of thought was going. It was nice to feel alive again. Nice to wake up in the morning looking forward to what the day might bring, instead of being trapped in an unpleasant job, that of an insurance investigator, spying on people making claims.

She was travelling light, only two suitcases packed mostly with new clothes. The lady in the charity shop was really grateful for Maggie's entire wardrobe which included several suits, numerous blouses and skirts and casual wear for when she had to blend in on a case.

Her boss told her that if she ever felt like returning, she was welcome seeing she was their best investigator.

All that unpaid overtime she'd put in disproving cases for them, no wonder they didn't want to lose her.

She'd saved them pots of money except for that last case: the little girl who wanted to go to Disneyland. She'd been knocked off her bike and a leg injury caused her to walk with a limp. The driver was never found. But then, as luck would have it, the father tripped in a supermarket over a box a shelf stacker had left in an unsafe place.

He claimed he suffered with back pain and had difficulty walking some days.

Grossly exaggerated of course, but when Maggie interviewed him and he said his little girl wanted to go to Disneyland, it struck a chord with her.

She congratulated herself for the one good thing she had done in the whole of her career. Bent the rules for the first time in her life and brought happiness to one little girl, and thanks to that she got a wake-up call.

Time for change. She grinned as she drove her downsized car into the driveway of Forge Cottage.

After unloading her belongings, she sat back in the car and drove the short distance back into town. A bottle of champagne for celebration purposes was on top of her shopping list.

The flower shop looked cheerful, she noted, and it was right across the road from *The Crier*.

The proprietor placed the pot plants Maggie had chosen into a cardboard box and introduced herself. "I'm Pattie Flowers," she said.

"That name really ties in with your line of business," Maggie smiled.

"Andrew Digwell and Alan Titchmarsh are good connecting names too," Pattie joked.

"I'm Maggie Lehane, and no, my name doesn't tie in with my business," Maggie held her hand out.

Pattie shook Maggie's hand. "Pleased to meet you," she said.

"Passing through, are you?"

"No, actually I'm the new owner of the place across the road and Forge Cottage is thrown in as well. Although it was the other way around," Maggie replied.

"So, are you going to get the paper going again?"

"Was it successful?" Maggie asked.

"Deaths, births and marriages and the usual advertising for local businesses, that's what kept it going. I used to write an article for it myself from time to time."

"On gardening," Maggie guessed.

"A glorified rag it might have been but people bought it, just in case there might be some news in it," Pattie laughed.

"Quiet town, so…"

"Nothing ever happens in this sleepy town."

"Court cases; did they report those?"

"Parking fines and non-payment of television licenses were hardly worth wasting ink on, but they did." Pattie smiled, revealing her small pearly white teeth.

Maggie handed over a ten euro note. "There's a lot to be said for a crime-free town," Maggie remarked.

"On the house," Pattie insisted.

Maggie was pleased with the welcoming present. "Thank you so much," she said.

"We should get together for a drink," Pattie suggested as she held the door open for Maggie.

"I'll take you up on that," Maggie called over her shoulder.

Maggie placed the box on the footpath and searched for her keys. Why was it that keys always disappeared into a black hole in your bag when you needed them most?

Suddenly she was aware of a tall figure towering over her. He was wearing a hoodie and immediately her vivid imagination went into overdrive. She was going to be mugged.

Miraculously the keys surfaced and Maggie tried to look calm as she opened the car boot.

The man wearing the hoodie picked up the box and carefully placed it in the car boot.

Why had she panicked? This was a small town, not a city. Things were civilized here, she scolded herself.

She headed across the road to *The Crier*, which was nestled between a chemist and a dry cleaners.

She nearly fell over the pile of envelopes and leaflets as she stepped into *The Crier*. She hadn't looked at it when she'd bought the cottage because it was enough to get her head round the idea of a geographical change.

She made her way down the hall and stopped at a door sporting the plaque 'Editor's Office'.

She took in the scene for a moment. There were a lot of papers on the desk, work-in-progress so to speak. It looked as though a pause button had been pressed and the editor had taken himself outside for a cigarette or cup of tea.

The reality was that he had suffered a heart attack right here.

She sat down on the leather chair and studied the papers on the desk.

Nothing exciting, just notices of things going on in neighbouring villages, like fetes and pub singing competitions. Homegrown vegetables, freshly made cakes and scones for sale at the Saturday market on the square in town, and other mundane happenings.

There was a file marked 'employees'. They were working part time and paid by the hour. Where were they now, she wondered as she tucked the file into her handbag without thinking and emerged out onto the street.

"I am so sorry."

She looked into the face of the bearded man who'd bumped into her and caused her to drop her bunch of keys.

He pressed the keys into her hand. "No harm done," she assured him.

"I know I am being cheeky, but is *The Crier* starting up again?"

She noticed the look of disappointment on his face when she said a definite no.

What she didn't notice was that the hoodie she'd previously encountered was lurking in the doorway of the dry cleaners, and he was as disappointed as the bearded man.

CHAPTER 3

Detective Inspector Robert Carroll searched the pockets of his leather jacket until he found a crumpled packet of cigarettes. "Well, what have we got here?" he said.

"A murder, sir," James Sayder answered.

"*Tu es con*," Robert muttered under his breath.

James pretended he hadn't heard but he had, and he knew enough French to know he'd just been called an idiot.

Robert pointed to the body with his cigarette. "Well, you wouldn't have to be a scientist to work out what's gone on here, would you now? The man's throat's been cut, and his hands – what's left of them, that is – are nailed to the desk."

James knew he was being rebuked but managed to remain expressionless.

"Nor would you even need to have a brain in your head to know that that's a feat he could hardly have accomplished himself. Which would rule out suicide, wouldn't you say?" Robert laughed sarcastically, pushed the cigarette packet back into one of his pockets and repeated the searching process until he located his lighter.

James Sayder, who happened to be the superintendent's nephew, was on summer break from Trinity College where he was studying law.

His uncle had kindly offered to give him work experience and Robert had been delegated to take James in hand. Robert was convinced the lad was a plant, and more than likely under instructions to run to Uncle Super with reports of everything going on.

Robert was well aware he would be labelled as paranoid if he voiced his suspicions. He'd also be told he was full of self-importance to think such a thing. The fact of the matter was he was in the super's bad books at the moment, and he had no choice but to go along with this nephew thing to prevent further grief.

No one said he had to be nice to the lad though.

Robert hated well-to-do brats, and their arrogance. He made no secret of his feelings, and it was for this very reason the super was currently mad at him.

There had been an incident a few weeks back. A few smart-alec college boys, home for the weekend, had carried out wanton acts of vandalism in the town centre. They were pissed out of their minds, but that was no excuse.

The super had given them a caution, nothing more than a gentle slap on the wrist. They were told never to do it again, like naughty little schoolboys.

If they'd been the sons of ordinary working-class people, Robert felt sure they would have been given a more heavy-handed punishment. It didn't go down too well when he had been forward enough to point it out to the boss.

The super defended the hooligans, saying it was just a harmless prank. He wouldn't want to offend their fathers who were probably his golfing cronies, Robert had concluded.

Had Robert realized that the upper-crust hooligans were going to get off so lightly, he'd have taken it upon himself to kick the shit out of them and to hell with the consequences.

His own father had operated like that when he was in the force, and it worked then. But in reality that was then, and this was now; and unfortunately the age of litigation had reared its ugly head.

These louts were the money crowd and they could buy themselves out of anything in this sleepy little town. The super told him to stop whinging about a few lousy trees and keep his head down like everyone else in the station.

Robert fingered his lighter, he was trying to give up smoking for a while now and it was driving him crazy. He had tried gum and patches, all to no avail, though according to a successful quitter at the station the only thing for it was to go cold turkey.

He'd come to regret sharing his attempts to give up the weed with the quitter, because every time he saw the chap he'd want to know Robert's progress. Three days was the longest he'd lasted, and he sure made up for lost time on the fourth day, smoking twice as many as he normally would.

"I'm afraid I don't smoke, sir." James Sayder broke in on Robert's thoughts.

"What?" Robert snapped, wondering what James was alluding to.

"Your lighter, sir, is it broken?"

"No, it's not," Robert said sharply. He was not going to get caught out again. No way would he be telling this young fellow about the quitting thing. It was bad enough having one chap on your back.

"The victim's name is Judge Mangan and he appears to have bled to death, sir," James furnished some more obvious information.

Robert forgave himself for yet another nicotine relapse. He was in the third week of putting up with this long-haired lapdog, and if ever he needed a fix it was right now, else he'd have to give the fellow a slap in the gob.

Show him the ropes, the super had said, but there wasn't anything to show. Nothing happened, not even a robbery, or more vandalism even. Not one iota, until now.

A murder in Magnerstown. Who'd have thought something like that would happen in the confines of the dullest place in the country?

There had been manslaughter twenty years previously, but it couldn't be compared with this brutal slaying.

Robert knew all about the manslaughter case because they were still talking about it in the station. The victim was an elderly man on holidays from England. He was only three days in town when he got involved in a fight after a night's drinking in a pub. The poor unfortunate choked to death on his false teeth. The body had been dumped down the alleyway behind the pub. Thankfully the perpetrator was caught and punished due to the testaments of a few conscientious witnesses who bravely came forward. They ignored threats from the hard man and gave damning evidence. So, like a lot of hard men, the thug made the one fatal mistake that was to be his undoing. He went too far.

He got eight years inside, a pittance for taking a life when all was said and done. On his release from prison, he moved abroad and was never heard of again. None of the locals wanted him back in their midst anyway. If he did it once, he could do it again, so they were well rid of him.

A plaque was erected in memory of the victim by the publican. He felt he should make amends because he felt responsible for what happened despite the heartfelt assurances from the townspeople and police that it was not his fault. It wasn't as if the holiday maker had been served too much drink, he should have been able to handle himself. It was terrible tough luck that he had a difference of opinion with the villain, but he wasn't to know the dire consequences which would ensue as a result of a really bad choice.

Robert lit his cigarette before realizing what he'd done.

The 'No Smoking' sign couldn't have been any bigger, the red lettering appearing two dimensional; it all but reached out and slapped him across the face. How could he have had a temporary memory lapse about the bloody smoking thing, after all those months of warning that the ban would finally be brought into law on this very day? Quickly he quenched the cigarette between his finger and thumb.

James jerked his head in the direction of the sign. "It'll take time to kick in."

Robert wanted to tell James to shut the fuck up but knew he couldn't really be that nasty to him, even though he was dying to put him in his place.

"Do you think the murderer was making a statement?" James once again broke in on his thoughts.

"How do you mean?" Robert indulged him.

"He has nailed the judge's hands down, which wouldn't have killed him, so there must be a message in that."

"You've been watching too much CSI, young man." Robert laughed and made his way out into the yard. He just had to have a cigarette, and they were still waiting for Dr Morris, who was by the looks of it, taking his bloody time.

CHAPTER 4

Joey Tyrell pushed his way into his small but adequate kitchenette. First things first, he thought as he placed his six-pack of vintage cider on the top shelf of the fridge. Next on the agenda was a roll-up cigarette out of the nice fresh tobacco pouch he'd just bought in the newsagents.

He loved Wednesdays because it was payday, in other words, collecting his jobseeker's allowance at the post office. He got that black-haired witch again today. She always looked at him like he was a scrounger getting paid out her own pocket. Next week he'd stand back and let the next punter ahead.

The bevies and tobacco for cigarettes always topped his shopping list, and why not? A man had to have some pleasures in life.

He thought about his brief encounter with the new owner of *The Crier* and his disappointment when she said the paper would not be restarting. Would there be anything he could do to change her mind?

The news about the city woman who'd bought Forge Cottage would spread like wildfire. Anything that went on in Magnerstown became common knowledge, sometimes before it even happened. It was that kind of in-your-face place, but despite all that, he loved his hometown. He'd never had an urge or inclination to spread his wings and travel. Home bird was the definition for his ilk. There were so many home birds in town that it was like one massive nest. Magnerstown, the Nest in the West.

He stubbed out his roll-up in the ashtray and made his way to his studio, as he proudly referred to it.

His best photos were framed and mounted on the walls. The ones he'd got prizes for still bore the rosettes.

Photography was his first passion and next in line was his painting, landscapes were his speciality.

He'd been thinking about compiling a book of photos but hadn't come up with a theme yet. He had come up with a title which, even if he said so himself, was ingenious.

Third Eye. Now, wasn't that some title! Didn't some Chinaman once say that the start of a long journey begins with the first step? They were on the ball those Chinese.

His train of thought continued as he made his way to the bathroom. He had loved working at *The Crier* though. It had given him a sense of purpose, and he was so alert when he was there.

His present predicament was dire. He felt jaded all the time, sometimes he stayed in bed half the day. What was the point in getting up, when there was nothing to do? Other days he'd be all fired up. He'd start a painting and get really stuck in, but halfway through he'd get a fit of the negativities.

He stared at his reflection in the mirror. A small trim of the beard now and then sufficed, but the hair. The sprinkling of grey was making him look about twenty years older, though the barber always said it made him look distinguished. It was like he had highlights, people paid good money for those. Joey couldn't help thinking the fellow was taking the piss with his next observation.

'You look like Richard Burton. Exactly like him if he had longer curlier hair.'

Joey had pleaded with the barber to dye his hair back to its original colour. The guy just laughed and said, 'You would look like a cat had taken up residence on top of your head.'

Maybe he should just trust the man. Another barber would grab the chance to put money in the till.

Yes, it had to be the right advice. Hair was the guy's trade after all, and his was photography. He was dwelling too much on things that wouldn't even bother him if he was out there, with a purpose.

But what would make the city woman change her mind about *The Crier*? Some kind of sensational breaking news it would have to be, something absolutely spectacular. A mind-blowing event would do it. That's a laugh, he mused. There was no chance of anything happening in this town.

There was only one thing to be done, have a can of cider and work out some kind of plan.

He got most of his best ideas while under the influence. You could call it a working liquid lunch.

He was so clever that sometimes he actually frightened himself.

CHAPTER 5

Maggie poured out a large glass of red wine and glanced at the bag of vegetables on the worktop. Vegetable stir-fry was the intention for her meal, but now she was having second thoughts. She took a generous mouthful of wine for motivation.

A takeaway would be less effort; she struggled with her laziness. She couldn't weaken and give in, so even if she had to force herself, the new health regime was clearly on the agenda.

She'd purchased her first non-stick wok, and a packet of utensils consisting of two bamboo spatulas of different sizes and a rice paddle. According to the label, the utensils would withstand continual dishwashing, and more importantly they would not scratch surfaces. Good news for Mr Wok, so. She took another mouthful of wine.

Further reading told her bamboo has been used by the Chinese in cooking for thousands of years.

She studied the recipe: ten minutes preparation time, and ten minutes cooking time.

She'd allow herself to finish the wine first and then get down to the chopping slicing and dicing. No rush.

Her mind drifted back to her conversation with Pattie Flowers, and the man she'd bumped into who wanted to know if *The Crier* would be back in business. Funny that, was he one of the former employees? She should have asked him what his interest was, and more importantly, who he was. At least he showed an interest in *The Crier*, unlike Pattie who was completely negative about it.

Maggie crossed the hall to the living room. Might as well have the rest of the wine in comfort, she rationalized, as she flopped down onto the settee.

She marvelled at the peace and quiet, she should have done this years ago. The sound of a loud thud in the hall broke the silence. Something had been pushed through the letterbox. The post had already been, so it couldn't be that. Maybe it was sales literature, she reasoned as she made her way out into the hall. She'd have to get one of those no junk mail stickers.

The contents of the large brown envelope proved very interesting. There were three glossy photographs. The first photo focused on a man looking out of a car window. The lady talking to him was the highlight of the next shot. And finally, from a different angle altogether, there was a plaque showing the name of the street.

There was a typed accompaniment with the heading 'He who Judges.' Seemingly the man in the car was the local judge, and he apparently was no stranger to a certain red light district in a place not too far away. The photos were proof positive, and could be used in evidence. They could also be used in another capacity, if a body felt brave enough to tell the story.

Maggie felt annoyance well up inside her. It was so true of these pillars of society characters, doling out punishment to people while they themselves were not entirely blameless. She had seen it so often, perverts, wife beaters and such like in jobs where they towered over misfortunates. Ruling with their iron fists, while their own private crimes went unnoticed. Someone should stand up and alert the public to these parasites. Whoever had gathered this information had started the ball rolling, and it would be a shame to lie back and do nothing.

Maggie opened the employees file she'd taken from *The Crier*. Mossie Harrington was listed as the typesetter.

Hurriedly she dialled the number.

A quiet-sounding man answered the phone.

"Are you Mossie Harrington?"

"Yes, that's me."

"I'm the woman who bought Forge Cottage and the newspaper business," Maggie started to explain.

"Are you going to start the paper up again?" There was a hint of excitement in the voice at the other end.

"Could I meet you?"

"Are you at the cottage now?"

"Yes, but I can meet you at a pub somewhere, it wouldn't take me long to get there," Maggie offered.

"No."

Maggie felt a stab of disappointment.

"I'd prefer to come to your place if you don't mind."

"Great." Maggie's spirits lifted.

Fifteen minutes later Mossie Harrington arrived at Forge Cottage.

Mossie Harrington was a completely different man to the one Maggie had conjured up in her mind's eye. She had expected a small mild-mannered man. Instead, a large burly figure of a man stood on her doorstep.

"Would you like something to eat, a sandwich maybe?" Maggie offered as he stepped inside.

"No thanks," Mossie declined. "I've just had my dinner, and to be honest it was a bigger one than usual. I've no room for anything else at the moment."

Maggie beckoned him to follow her into the sitting room, but stopped when she noticed he'd stalled.

"Could I ask a bit of a favour?" Mossie said.

"Go on, ask."

"It's my dog. He's outside, you see, and I'm afraid he might get scared and run away. Would you allow him into the hall? He'll be no trouble, I promise." Mossie sounded nervous.

Maggie couldn't help smiling at the simplicity of the request. "Of course," she agreed.

Once inside, Mossie's dog settled down after getting a reassuring pat on the head from his owner.

"What's his name?" Maggie asked.

"Sparky."

"Can I give him something to eat, or drink even?"

"Thanks, but he's grand," Mossie assured her.

After settling himself on the settee, Mossie studied the contents of the big brown envelope.

"Would you like a drink? I've beer in the fridge."

Mossie informed her he didn't drink and then turned his attention back to the business in hand.

He seemed deeply interested and that pleased Maggie.

"The slimy old judge, eh?" Mossie finally said.

"You know him?"

"Everyone knows that old bastard. His house is up the road, about a ten-minute walk from here. It's the place with the high walls and green metal gate."

"Yes, I've noticed it, there are loads of trees."

"Yeah, that's the place."

"Is the information true, do you think?" Maggie asked.

"The dogs in the street know that," Mossie said.

"You can't be serious," Maggie said.

Mossie looked her straight in the eye. "But tell me this and tell me no more."

"Yes."

"Are you thinking of running the story?"

Maggie felt anxious. "Do you think it would be a bit foolhardy? Could it be libellous?" she asked.

"Can't be libellous if it is true, can it? But then that slimy snake in the grass merchant might be able to get around that one."

"And then again he might not," Maggie reasoned.

"There's something you should know," Mossie said.

"What?"

"There was a body found in the courthouse."

"You are not going to tell me it is him."

"That's the rumour."

"He can't sue us for libel then. So we could be looking at a unique event in the history of the press. Starting up and finishing in the same week," Maggie announced.

"The paper is defunct anyway," Mossie reminded her. "So, what's it to be then, resuscitation or burial? Will it be third-time lucky?"

"How do you mean third-time lucky?"

"It was once a great business, used to print several provincial papers from around the county, and then it went bust. That's where your man, owner of Forge Cottage came in. He bought it and turned it into the local rag, known as *The Crier*," Mossie said.

"That explains the printing press then, I thought it was a bit elaborate for a local paper. I used to work for a magazine one time, I have a bit of experience in the printing world, you could say," Maggie explained.

"That's a help," Mossie said. "You must know all about deadlines."

"I am going to make a snap decision on this," Maggie said.

"Is it a before you change your mind sort of thing?" Mossie asked.

"Would you be interested in coming on board?" Maggie ventured.

"Yes, but there's one condition," Mossie warned.

Maggie felt a request for a wage rise coming on, and said so.

"I don't care about the money," Mossie assured her. "I'd even work for nothing."

"We couldn't have that," Maggie smiled.

"It's Sparky I'm worried about. Could I bring him to work with me?"

Maggie sighed with relief. "Is that all you want?"

"He's getting on, you see. My wife died last year and I don't like leaving him alone," Mossie explained. "He'd be no trouble, I promise."

"Of course you can bring him in with you," Maggie agreed. "But I'm not paying him wages."

Mossie stuck his hand out. "Let's shake on it then."

"Deal."

"Is the chap who did the photography still around?" Maggie asked. She had no idea she'd already met him outside *The Crier* and hadn't given the poor fellow the answer he wanted to hear.

"You mean Joey Tyrell, the multitask man? There was no end to his talents. Photography, reporting, you name it." Mossie laughed.

"He sounds great."

"He's taken up painting, not walls now mind you," Mossie said.

"Art."

"He sells the odd picture now and then. It's a good job he's got his social security payments to back him up, otherwise he'd starve to death, the poor article. You'll like him, though. He's a bit effeminate, but you won't hold that against him, I'm sure."

"Would you contact him for me?"

"I will," Mossie promised. "And I can tell you, without a shadow of a doubt, that he'll certainly come on board. He lived and died for *The Crier*, so he did."

"I must buy a painting from him," Maggie said.

"He excels in photography. He won prizes for some of his pictures."

Maggie was surprised at that revelation. "He won't be expecting big wages now, will he?"

"He'll be so glad to be working again he'll do it for nothing." Mossie laughed as he made his way out into the hall.

Maggie bent down to pat Sparky on the head. "We'll give it our best shot then, won't we, Sparky?" she said.

CHAPTER 6

As the house came into view at the end of a long driveway, Robert was reminded of the place in France where he'd worked in the early days of his time there.

It was a farm miles away from nowhere and he had laboured for two years for small money. The money didn't matter really, he had a nice room all to himself and he was as happy as he could be.

He had left Ireland out of boredom, but unfortunately found himself still bored, although the fact that he was in a different place seemed to make it more palatable.

His father was livid when he'd announced he was emigrating.

'Are you mad? You're throwing away a good career that you've trained for? Do you realize there are young men who would kill for your job?' He could still hear the angry words. He remembered his own reaction too. 'Who the hell would kill for a job with the cops? They are hated, aren't they? Everyone says so.'

He'd spent eleven years in France, muddling along from day to day, job to job, until he met Annie. She had enough ambition for the two of them. It had been her idea to return to Ireland, and he found himself giving in and moving home to Magnerstown. He got back on the force, and Annie started working in Cliff's Restaurant. She had a plan. Save and gain credibility with the local bank, so she could secure a loan in order to start her own business.

She had a plan for Robert too. He would work his way up to the top like his father before him, she'd enthused; and he'd be the superintendent.

He wanted to tell her he'd prefer to sweep the roads rather than take up that job, but he'd decided to let her have her dream and go along with it for a quiet life.

James surveyed the gates that cut Green Park off from the rest of the world. "This place is like Fort Knox," he said, clearly impressed.

Robert looked at the sprawling mansion. "Too big for one old bastard," he said.

"Where will we start?" James asked.

Robert pointed to the first heavy oak door in the hall. "Sitting room first, I take it this is it." His hunch was right, and James congratulated him as they made their way into the large room which was furnished with oversized bookcases, and ugly, bulky, dark furniture which, despite its lack of appeal, was antique and worth a fortune.

There were pictures on the wall, portraits of men and women from a bygone age, and one of the house, also in past times.

James held up a dusty finger which he'd run along the top of the white marble mantelpiece. "He could have done with a good housekeeper."

Robert laughed. "You're like that programme on television, how to clean your house."

"It's how clean."

"What?"

"It's 'How Clean is Your House?'" James corrected.

"Whatever, same difference, isn't it?" Robert snapped. "So how clean is your house, James?" Robert asked.

James ignored Robert's sarcastic question and studied the shelves and sideboards.

"Don't seem to be any sign of personal stuff like family photos," James noted.

Robert pulled out a few drawers to make himself look busy.

"Men have no interest in soft things like that. It's usually the women who provide the personal touches, and our Judge Mangan hadn't a woman, had he? He never married, according to those in the know," Robert remarked.

"That's really sad," James said.

Robert made to leave the room. "Nothing wrong with being unmarried," he said gruffly.

The rest of the house threw up nothing interesting either, except for a few letters with a South African postmark from a Sister Mary Aloysius. They had been tucked away in the drawer of the judge's bedside locker.

Robert handed the letters over to James. "I bet they're begging letters, with the usual old plea about the need for money to save souls in Africa."

James started to read out one of the letters. "Dear Cornelius," he began.

"Cornelius, was that his name?" Robert sneered.

"It would seem so." James continued to scan the letters in silence.

"Well, anything of note?" Robert asked.

"There's no mention of looking for money, just everyday stuff like the weather, and pains and aches, and getting old," James said.

Robert moved off towards the window and looked out onto the lawn below. In his mind, he was back in France in the farmhouse where all the workers, otherwise known as the *ouvrier agricole*, sat at one table at mealtimes. The owner and his mini-mes sat at the other table.

"This place reminds you of somewhere, does it not, sir?"

Robert swung round. "You're very perceptive, aren't you, young James?"

"I do my best, sir," James replied.

"That talent won't go astray in the law business. Are you going to represent good or bad people?"

"There's more money to be got out of bad people," James answered.

"So, am I right in thinking your father is a barrister and you will be following in his footsteps?"

"Yes, he's a barrister; he practices in America."

"America!"

"He met an American woman when he was at college, they were great friends, but after a drunken night out while she was off somewhere else, he ended up in bed with my mother and managed to make her pregnant."

Robert was taken aback by the revelation of such private matters, but then the youth of today were noted for wearing their hearts on their sleeves. They liked being up front.

"He did the honourable thing of course and married my mother, but Miss America was always there in the background, waiting and biding her time until he returned to her patient arms. So it came as no surprise when he eventually scarpered off to America with her."

"I'm sorry," Robert said. Despite James's brave statement, he detected a hint of hurt in his voice. The man was his father after all, and a father's job is to father; yet this man wasn't doing his duty, the selfish toe rag.

"By the way, sir, our house is quite clean. I had to see to it when my mother developed the three Bs but she's fine now, thankfully."

"The three Bs," Robert echoed.

"Bed, booze and bereft," James explained.

"You know, sometimes desperate measures have to be taken in order to work things through," Robert observed.

"There's nothing in any of the letters, sir, just the same old small talk." James returned the bundle to the drawer and closed it carefully.

"That's life isn't it, really? One long litany of small talk." Robert laughed softly. "Blah blah and bloody blah."

James's face folded into sympathetic mode.

"I'm more in the need of a cigarette than sympathy," Robert grunted. He swept past James and made his way out into the fresh air.

He hated this place, hated the way it stirred up old memories that he thought he'd erased from his mind. All he wanted to do was exist from day to day, going from 'a' to 'b' with the minimum of fuss. Surely that wasn't too bloody much to expect.

CHAPTER 7

Mossie poked his head round the office door. "There's a detective inspector here to see you, he said his name is Robert Carroll."

Maggie was not in the mood for some old fart coming to reprimand her because she'd disclosed the truth about the judge.

"Show him in." Maggie winked at Mossie and braced herself for the onslaught.

She was mildly surprised to see that the detective did not fit her pre-conceived old fart notion. By the look of him he was just a few years older than her and actually quite handsome – much as she hated to admit it. She wasn't allowed to notice things like that, she scolded herself. She was supposed to be off men.

"What do you think you're playing at?" he said.

Maggie detected a hint of underlying anger. He had a copy of *The Crier* in his hand and his fingers were digging right into it with a vengeance.

"I take it you're referring to our front-page story," Maggie said. She was adamant she was not going to allow herself to be drawn into conflict.

Robert threw the paper onto the desk. The way he stared at her made her feel really uncomfortable. "I'd like to know where you got your information from and why you decided to print this fairy story, because that's all it is," he said.

"It's the stuff people need to be made aware of because there's too much crap going on behind closed doors. These two-faced hypocrites need to be exposed for what they are, and I'm all for that." Maggie felt proud of herself for standing up to the oaf of a detective in front of her. That's exactly what he was, an arrogant good-looking oaf. She cringed for noticing again.

"So, you believe your sources, do you?" Robert retorted.

Maggie managed to keep her cool. "The camera never lies," she said.

"You have no scruples printing something about a man who can't defend himself—"

"Good job he's dead; I doubt if I would have got his permission." Maggie was still in control, that's how she was going to play it: calm, cool and collected.

Robert gave her a patronizing look.

"You are talking about a man who dished out punishment to misfortunates in court, a man who acted like he was squeaky clean. Did he allow these persons to defend themselves?" Maggie said.

"Maybe you did speak to him, and maybe he told you he'd sue you for libel if you went ahead with your cock-and-bull story," Robert suggested.

"Don't be ridiculous," Maggie snapped. The detective was getting right up her nose with his outrageous suggestions, and she was fast losing patience.

"And of course you went ahead with your story, because you people are so full of your own self-importance," Robert continued.

"I'd have thought that title was more fitting for you." Maggie laughed at the irony of his statement.

"You people have no conscience." Robert was not going to let up.

"Give me a break." Maggie had tired of the rebuking. "If you have something constructive to say would you mind getting on with it? Because I am rather busy." Maggie quickly got back to her calm self. She would not allow him to goad her into losing her temper, which was probably his plan. He would keep working on her until she'd say something she'd regret.

"The fact of the matter is Judge Mangan has been found dead."

Maggie looked the detective in the face. "Heart attack was it?"

"No."

Maggie felt a pang of guilt. The old bastard hadn't committed suicide, had he? And no doubt she'd be blamed for it, wouldn't she? They'd need a scapegoat to pin his untimely demise on, and it looked as if she was the chosen one, the sacrificial lamb. Still, they wouldn't be able to charge her with anything even if he had committed suicide. It wasn't as if she had put his head in a noose, or made him swallow a bucket of tablets, or whatever method it was he'd chosen to do away with himself.

"I'm investigating a murder."

Maggie was completely taken aback. The pervert had been murdered. This was serious stuff.

"So, why are you here? Am I a suspect?"

Robert ignored the question and made an observation instead. "So, there's another front-page story in the making for your little rag."

"Yes, the paper has indeed come back with a bang," Maggie said.

Despite her bravado, the judge getting murdered was the last thing she'd expected. But who could possibly have carried out such a thing, and why? Maggie's mind was racing with questions.

"I need to know where you got your information from," Robert said.

"You know I'm not going to tell you that."

* * *

Robert wondered if he was sitting in front of a woman who would do anything to make *The Crier* a success. Could she stoop to murder? She did look surprised about Mangan's untimely death. She could be faking that. She could have practiced the innocence and surprise.

Maggie gave a knowing wink. "The dogs in the street gave me the information about the judge."

Robert's need for a nicotine fix was the reason he brought the meeting to a close. "I'll be in touch," was his parting shot. He made for the door and quickly let himself out.

"Aren't you going to ask me not to leave the country?" Maggie shouted after him.

He could hear the laughter in her voice, she was taking the piss and he knew it. He wasn't going to fight back, not this time. He'd wait until he had something concrete to land on her doorstep, and he'd enjoy watching her trying to talk her way out of it. Bloody woman, who did she think she was, editor of the *Daily Mirror*?

She wasn't wearing any rings on her fingers, he'd noticed. She was hardly married, was she? Robert laughed at the thoughts that were running through his head. Why should he care whether she was married, divorced or engaged? Who in their right mind would want her, with a temper like that? No, he shouldn't really say that about her, she was a little bit mad with him alright, but she managed to keep it in check. It was he who had the temper to be honest about it. What had got into him? It wasn't as if he gave a tuppenny fuck about the old judge. It was just his job to interview Miss Lehane about the whole sorry affair. Find out where she got her information for the article from if she was willing to disclose it, which she wasn't, as it turned out. And that was OK, freedom of the press and all that malarkey. If he was to be honest about it she was right when she said the dogs in the street knew Judge Mangan was a dirty old git. She took an awful chance printing the story, though. There could have been huge repercussions. She was lucky, but the judge wasn't.

Who killed him anyway, and why? It was going to be very interesting finding out the answer to that one.

A murder here in Magnerstown, he still hadn't got his head round it. With all the thoughts swirling around in his head, he hadn't realized he had stamped out the half-smoked cigarette underfoot. He picked it up and half-walked, half-ran to the litter bin which was affixed to a pole some yards away and dropped it in.

He wasn't finished yet. He removed the cigarette packet from his pocket and crushed it before throwing it with so much force at the bin, but it bounced off the metal and landed on the ground.

As he stormed off up the street, the thought crossed his mind that he hadn't been this fired up for years.

CHAPTER 8

Sister Mary Immaculate's Nursing Home had been in its heyday a boarding school for girls run by nuns, hence its idyllic setting in the heart of twenty acres of land on one of the approach roads to Magnerstown. Its grounds were well landscaped, and there was an abundance of beautiful trees of oak, beech and maple, which added their own aesthetic appeal to the place.

Now and then, some writer or actress from England, Scotland or Wales would appear on a chat show panel on television revelling in the fact that they were proud past pupils of Mary I's as it was affectionately christened by the boarders. These celebrities would then go on to extol its virtues by thanking most profusely Sister Mary This, or Sister Mary That, for the grounding and nurturing of their talents.

Evidence of the school's past life still remained in the form of religious statues both in the grounds and inside the building itself. The tiny chapel was for the use of patients who felt fit enough to attend Fr. Scully's Mass at twelve noon every Sunday. Afterwards the priest dined in the private quarters reserved for the matron. It was an arrangement that suited him, because it cut out having to forage for himself back at the priest's house. He had never indulged in the luxury of employing a housekeeper like some of his contemporaries. Some parishioners said this could be due to meanness, while others said he was a down-to-earth no-nonsense man, and great credit was due to him for his independence.

* * *

Greg Joubert almost collided with the priest who was just leaving after his Sunday stint at the nursing home. He apologized grudgingly, like it was the priest's fault for getting in the way.

Greg was on a mission, he was in a hurry to get to Mary Hammond's room with the big news. He felt like an excited child racing home after one of his adventures and bursting to blurt it all out like he used to do years ago.

After kissing her on the cheek, Greg stood back to look at her. "You must be feeling better today, Ma," he remarked. He was alluding to the fact that she was sitting on the big comfortable red armchair beside her bed.

Mary Hammond did not reply. If she did, it would be a miracle, because Mary couldn't speak, and it wasn't known if this was the result of a stroke or some other underlying medical condition. No previous records relating to her medical state had been handed over when she first arrived at the nursing home. Despite her misfortunes, she was comfortable in Mary I's. The nickname had remained despite the change of inhabitants.

Mary was safe for the first time in her life, and even though she couldn't convey it, her relaxed attitude said it all. Mary I's was her home of eleven years now, thanks to the Health Board closing down that dreadful institution where she'd been imprisoned for several years.

"I have something to tell you," Greg announced. He was trembling in anticipation of her reaction.

Mary's pale blue eyes flickered in acknowledgement.

"Judge Mangan is dead." Greg searched her face for some kind of happy response, but she remained stone-faced.

"He was murdered," Greg revealed.

Realizing she didn't appear to be taking in his big revelation at all, he desperately repeated the words, more slowly this time.

A look of surprise appeared momentarily on Mary's face, intimating that she understood what she had just been told.

Greg took *The Crier* from his pocket, and offered to read it out to her.

Mary became agitated, and Greg knew from her body movements and face contortions that she did not want to hear the details. He felt instantly deflated, he had been so sure she would be really pleased, or maybe she was afraid of what it meant.

"Alright, Ma, I won't bother telling you the details." Greg rolled up the paper and put it back into his pocket.

"I brought some Yorkshire toffees for you," said Greg, quickly changing the subject. "You love those, don't you? I'll put them here on your locker for you."

Nurse Katie Manning stuck her head round the door. "Everything all right?" she asked. Noticing the look of unease on Mary's face she approached the chair.

"You alright, Mary?" she asked.

Stupid girl, Greg thought, asking his mother a question like she was going to answer it. The consultant that Greg had seen about his mother's physical condition had been brutally honest. He'd said that she would never talk or walk properly again, and she would have only limited use of her limbs, excepting a miracle, and Greg did not believe in those.

"Do you want to go to the toilet, Mary, is that it? Or maybe you'd like a drink, are you thirsty?" Nurse Manning was still probing.

Greg couldn't help but feel irritated by the interruption and struggled to control himself. Didn't the silly girl know that his mother wore the adult version of a nappy? Why was she mentioning toilets? Unless of course she was thinking of changing the thing, and wanted to save him embarrassment.

Greg suspected she'd formed the opinion he'd upset his mother, and she felt it her duty to get him out of the place. Whatever it was she was thinking, she was a snooty little cow, sticking her nose into people's private business.

"Let's see what the matter is." The nurse proceeded to remove the tartan rug covering Mary's lap.

Greg took the hint and leaned down to kiss his mother goodbye. "I'll see you tomorrow, Ma," he said. As he made for the door Nurse Manning called after him.

"I didn't mean to interrupt," she said.

"I was going anyway," he lied. He cursed her under his breath; he did not like that girl one bit. She was far too cute for her own good, and he hated the way she was always snooping around, watching him, like he was some kind of criminal or something.

He stormed out of the room before saying something he might regret. The nursing home had got well paid for his mother. A cheque had been paid up front by the Health Board on the day she was admitted. That payment covered her stay right up to the age of ninety, and more besides. No expense had been spared, and quite rightly so; they owed her big time after what she'd gone through in that horrible asylum they'd been subsidizing. Mary I's Nursing Home was struggling at the time of his mother's placement and the advancement for her stay was more than welcome, in fact the place could have closed down had it not been for Mary Hammond.

All the other patients were only paying their fees on a weekly basis, which made his mother special, didn't it, and here was that bitch of a nurse treating him like shit. He wanted to slap her into eternity, but he knew he'd have to play it cool. He hadn't seen his mother for eighteen years and he didn't want to jeopardize things now. He had uncovered a lot of what had happened to her while he'd been away. The more he was finding out about the suffering she'd endured, the more people he wanted to punish, and he was going to have no qualms about sorting them out either.

Ten years old was all he'd been when he was whisked off to Cape Town and fostered out to the Joubert's. He hadn't known it at the time, but within a few weeks of his departure, Mary Hammond had been admitted to that looney bin with a madman in charge. That crackpot Doctor Curtin had been using experimental drugs on the patients, and it all came out in the open when a patient crawled out onto a window ledge on the top floor. The poor man had to be scraped off the ground and shovelled into a black sack. It was then that the hue and cry began with the Health Board instigating a thorough investigation into what was going on in the institution, as if they didn't already know. They were turning a blind eye to the way the doctor was operating, because they didn't want the bother of repatriating the patients, but they were forced to act in the end.

Mary Hammond's qualification for entry to the institution was supposedly because she was off her head. Greg knew the real reason was because she had to be hidden away, she had simply become a liability.

A million times he'd played the disgusting scenes over in his head. A million times the picture of that bully of a man came into his head. The dirty scoundrel was constantly abusing his mother, pawing her with his big dirty hands. The sick bastard getting away with it time after time – that was the worst part of it all. She didn't like it. He knew by the way she protested, and often he'd hear her crying afterwards. She couldn't have told the authorities, she wouldn't have got very far seeing his father was such an important man. In all his innocence, Greg had once asked, 'Why don't you get him put in gaol?' She'd laughed and said it was something that would never happen, she was only the housekeeper, and nobody would believe her.

But it all became too much for Greg, he couldn't stand idly by any more, so he decided he would have to save the woman himself.

His father's secretary who lived in with them told him not to say such things when he appealed to her for help. She either didn't want to believe what was happening to his mother, or she knew it only too well and was keeping quiet because she wasn't going to jeopardize her job.

He should have killed him then, that bastard of a father of his, instead of just stabbing him in the hand with that silly old nail. But it was all he could do at the time. He was only a child back then, and no match for an adult. He wasn't a child now, no, he was a man and he had an awful lot of wrongs to right.

CHAPTER 9

"You're worth your weight in gold, Mossie," Maggie remarked.

"In that case I'm worth a fortune so." Mossie pointed to his stomach paunch.

"So, how's the diet going?" Maggie asked.

"Hit and miss," Mossie said.

"A minute on the lips, a lifetime on the hips; isn't that what they say?" Maggie said.

"I can vouch for that." Mossie tapped his hips.

"Joey Tyrell has finished the painting for me, he's hanging it up this very afternoon, as it happens," Maggie enthused.

"So, did you two finally agree on a subject?"

"Forge Cottage, and I'm really looking forward to seeing it."

Mossie shook his head. "Afternoon you say, I don't think so."

"Oh."

"He'll arrive at your door in the middle of the night to do the job. He'll be tanked up from cider and firing on all cylinders. He'll probably make a pass at you, he gets very lovey-dovey when he's drunk," Mossie teased.

Maggie laughed.

"No, I'm quite serious," Mossie said. "He's well known for it. There was a lady he fancied living at the end of his street."

"A lady you say."

"Every Friday night he'd arrive at her door whispering sweet nothings. No, I'm wrong, he didn't whisper because everybody in the street heard the carry-on of him."

"Oh well, there will be no neighbours to hear his ranting and ravings out at my place. I might even take him up on the offer," Maggie joked.

"You've nothing to fear," Mossie set her straight. "He's a kind of all talk and no action merchant, if you get what I mean," Mossie said.

"I've met one or two of them boys in my time," Maggie replied.

"But seriously, it's all an act with him, this woman chasing. I don't believe for one minute that he's ever even had one. He only goes so far, you see, and that could all be a front too. God knows what goes on in that little head of his. I don't think he even knows what sexuality he is, not that I'm suggesting anything untoward, you understand." Mossie gave a knowing wink.

"But he's quite harmless, I'm sure."

"Indeed he is," Mossie agreed. "Harmless."

"I've been thinking about our judge," Maggie said, changing the subject. "We should look over the court reports in the back numbers to see if he has upset somebody so badly in the past they'd want to kill him."

"Like giving someone a stiff prison sentence, you mean?" Mossie ventured.

"Or maybe throwing a case out of court, that kind of thing," Maggie deliberated.

"You think revenge is the reason he's been killed?"

"Well, it's just an option," Maggie replied.

"You could well have a point," Mossie said. "Someone he sent to gaol out for revenge, like something you'd see on the telly."

"There's a lot of fact in fiction, you know."

"I'll tell you something which might surprise you. I myself could fit your sentencing theory, except I didn't go to gaol," Mossie said quietly.

"You have a dark past, have you, Mossie?"

"Nothing spectacular now," he admitted.

"Come on, the suspense is killing me," Maggie said.

"It was serious enough I suppose, but it could have been disastrous, I was lucky I didn't kill someone. I was coming home from work, well, from the pub actually to be honest. We always went for a few pints on a Friday night to round off the week before leaving the city for home. I used to manage to drive all those miles afterwards without a hitch, except for one particular night when I must have had that one too many."

"I know the one," Maggie said.

"The minute I hit town it all went arseways," Mossie continued.

"You got arrested for drunk driving." Maggie was one step ahead.

"I was done for drunk driving alright, but not at a checkpoint. I crashed into a shop window on the main street. I couldn't believe what was happening. There I was, almost home, nice and easy with no hitches, but then I go and wake the cops up. They were probably having their usual snooze until the shop alarm went off. Even the dead couldn't sleep through the racket that thing made."

"So, that's the reason you don't drink now."

"I learned a very big lesson from that crazy little misadventure."

"So, what punishment did the judge dish out to you?" Maggie asked.

"Six months off the road was the going rate for that kind of offence at the time, only Judge Mangan decided he was going to make an example out of me – the miserable old shit. He disqualified me for five years."

"That was a bit steep. I mean, it wasn't as if you'd killed somebody."

"I'm talking fifteen years ago, there were no young fancy solicitors getting you off on a technicality then."

"Why didn't you appeal it?"

"There was nothing stopping anybody from appealing a heavy sentence or fine, but very few did, because the appeal judge usually gave out an even worse punishment; to pay you back for having the gall to question the actions of one of his counterparts."

"You're quite right about that," Maggie said. "I saw it happen several times during my last employment."

"It was a big blow to me financially, you know. I had to give up my job in the city and work here in Magnerstown for half the money. The sad thing was, the money mattered because my wife had just been diagnosed with cancer at the time, and she could have done without that kind of hardship on top of it all."

"The poor woman."

"Giving up the drink didn't come easy, it wasn't that I craved the stuff, but it was an escape from reality for a few hours. I had come to really depend on it; like an anaesthetic, you see. I needed to wipe out every emotion I was feeling. I was sick to death of myself and the world. I wanted to blot it all out, but I could never get away from myself. There I was, every morning, a big fat miserable waste of space looking into the mirror, cringing at the thoughts of having to put down another day on the planet. I knew I couldn't go on like that, so I decided I'd kick the habit; if not for myself then for the wife. She needed support during her treatment, and I owed her, big time."

"Must have been a tough time for you both," Maggie said.

"It took twelve long months of treatment and tests, tablets and potions before she recovered. So, just as it was all over, what did I do?"

"A relapse with the booze."

"I'd been facing my demons by going cold turkey you could say, and I got so depressed that I even contemplated suicide. I went into the pub and drank like something possessed. I don't know how many whiskeys I'd downed, but I had enough to make me go berserk and wreck the pub. The law was called, the men in white coats were called, they were all called," Mossie said.

"Yeah, that would do it alright, I can just imagine the whole thing, fire brigades, ambulances and overhead helicopters," Maggie joked.

"So I ended up in the infamous Renovatio, for my sins," Mossie said.

"Treatment centre?" Maggie asked.

"Not at all, it was a glorified mental institution, run by the only lunatic in the place, if I may say so, Dr Curtin, and his alternative medicine. I was there for six months before they let me out."

"That must have been an awful experience."

"It was a nightmare, so I needed someone to blame for it all, that's what you do when you're an alcoholic, you blame everyone but yourself. So every time I saw Mr High and Mighty, Judge Mangan, I wanted to trash the living daylights out of him, and I felt like that for a long time."

"I wouldn't blame you for wanting to do that under the circumstances."

"It took me ages to accept that I was my own worst enemy, and to come to the understanding that everything that had happened along the way was all for the best in the long run."

Maggie tapped Mossie lightly on the back and gave him a big congratulatory smile.

"It was the fear of being sent back into that hellhole, Renovatio, that helped me come to my senses and successfully give up the real cause of all my misfortunes, the worst thing that's ever been invented, that curse of a thing called alcohol."

"I wouldn't blame you if you felt some little pang of satisfaction when you heard Judge Mangan was dead," Maggie said.

"I'd got over my hatred for him, I had to, you see; I just couldn't let it continue eating me up. Instead of resenting him, I just prayed for the bastard like it is suggested in a certain kind of meeting I attend."

"AA," Maggie prompted.

"Yeah, but we're not supposed to say."

"Secret society, eh?"

"Something like that, yes," Mossie said.

"So you mustn't harbour grudges. That's the psychology of it."

"That's the idea, but I'll tell you something, when I heard the old shit was dead I allowed myself to jump up and down for one sweet minute."

"You danced a jig."

"Then I thought about the way he died, and that was a real bonus. I got another minute out of that." Mossie smiled broadly.

"It was a gory affair alright from the sounds of it, he must have suffered quite a bit," Maggie said.

"Oh, he suffered alright, he got his just desserts which were a long time coming, but he got them," Mossie replied.

"Yes, and wasn't it great that it all happened here, in Magnerstown? It's good news for us, and good news for them," Maggie said.

"Murder is the best kind of thing to sell newspapers. People have a ghoulish interest in things of that nature. They pour over every detail. There aren't too many who would admit to being that interested, but they do love it. They absolutely revel in it," Mossie said.

CHAPTER 10

Maggie and Pattie were led to a table for two by a smart young waiter at Cliff's Restaurant.

Maggie studied the black-and-white décor. "This place looks very nice," she said.

"And the owner is nice too, in fact he should be the dish of the day," Pattie said. She removed the pale blue silk scarf which was loosely knotted round her neck, and carefully placed it on the back of her chair.

"Dish of the day sounds great, but not much good if you happen to be a vegetarian." Maggie laughed.

Pattie smiled at the waiter as he presented them with the big black leather-encased menus with the words 'Cliff's Restaurant' embossed on them in fancy gold lettering.

"Are you not a meat eater then?" Pattie enquired as soon as the waiter breezed away leaving them to browse the menus at their leisure.

"I blow hot and cold on the matter. One month I'm meatless and the next I'm totally carnivorous, but tell me about this dish, Cliff," Maggie encouraged. "Just how meaty is he?"

"He's in his mid-forties, available, and absolutely filthy rich," Pattie disclosed.

Maggie nodded as she scanned the menu. "I can see why he's in the money, with the prices he's charging."

"But it is total class," Pattie said. "And you have to pay for that."

Maggie was beginning to form the opinion that Pattie was a bit of a snob in her own way.

"And you get such a nice clientele in here, no riff raff," Pattie went on.

More evidence of snobbery, Maggie thought. She gritted her teeth and said, "That's nice to know."

The waiter returned. "Are you ladies ready to order now?" he asked.

"I'll have the lamb with the Cashel Blue cheese sauce," Pattie said.

"And to start?" the young man prompted.

"Seared tuna and rocket salad with dressing on the side," Pattie gushed.

"And yourself, Madam, what would you like?" The waiter turned his attention to Maggie.

"I'll have the same, Pieter," Maggie said. The menu was so pompous she couldn't even be bothered to read it.

"Oh, so you know one another, you're a sly old dog, Maggie," Pattie said.

Maggie pointed to the waiter's badge. "It says Pieter," she said.

"Anything to drink, ladies?"

"Gin and tonic for me," Pattie said. "I'm not into wine really, how about you, Maggie?"

"I'm definitely into wine, so I'll have a glass of the house special chardonnay," Maggie said. She wondered if she was going to get on with Pattie after all. Would this be their first and last excursion out together?

"So, how was your week?" Pattie broke in on her thoughts.

"Busy."

"I must say you've done wonders with *The Crier*, you've brought it back from the dead; that's what everyone's saying," Pattie said.

"It's the dead we have to thank for the successes we're having, all we need now are a few more murders," Maggie joked.

"You've got some good features, apart from the murder, that is," Pattie replied.

The waiter arrived with the starters on two gleaming white square plates.

Maggie eyed the dish that had been set down in front of her. She couldn't help thinking that a magnifying glass would be handy to find the tuna. It appeared to be lost in the jungle of greenery.

"Wait till you taste it, it's absolutely divine." Pattie smacked her lips.

Maggie wondered if she'd ever get to taste the concoction at all. Every time she brought the fork up to her mouth, the tuna fell apart and landed back onto the jungle on her plate. Pattie on the other hand seemed to have no difficulty at all. Maybe she's had more practice, Maggie mused.

"You should do a feature on this place," Pattie said between chews.

"I'll think about it," Maggie lied.

"Look who's just walked in," Pattie whispered.

Robert Carroll seated himself at a table in the corner by the window and glanced around.

Catching his eye, Pattie waved hello.

For a split second Maggie's heart sank, she was afraid he was going to come over, but she needn't have worried. He appeared to be much too interested in the paper he was reading, and it wasn't *The Crier*, she noted. He had made it quite plain what he thought of that little effort when he came to her office.

"Do you know the detective well?" Maggie said.

"Do you want me to fill you in?" Pattie asked.

"It'll be something to talk about."

"You like him, don't you? Ah go on, admit it," Pattie said.

"No, I don't like him. As a matter of fact, I hate him if you must know, but tell me about him anyway."

"He was engaged. French she was. A fine tall good-looking woman with gorgeous black shiny hair. She worked here for Cliff, believe it or not."

"A waitress?" Maggie guessed.

"God no, she was the head chef."

Pattie took another forkful of her salad before continuing with the story. "Next thing we knew she'd upped and left after two years of hard graft. It was thanks to her that the restaurant became such a success."

Maggie was delighted to hear Robert got kicked in the teeth.

"It must have hit him hard, though he didn't show it. They met in France you know," Pattie said.

"Was it a holiday romance?" Maggie asked.

"Our mutual friend had been living there for twenty years or so. It was rumoured he'd had some kind of a run-in with his father, and that was the reason he went off in the first place."

"Or else it could be that he wanted to sow his wild oats in sunnier climes," Maggie suggested.

"Anyway, to cut a long story short he arrived back with Annie, that was her name by the way. All appeared to be going well, but as I said she just disappeared overnight. No one knew the reason, but I have my own ideas about it."

"You have?"

"She had an affair."

"So how long is it since they split up?" Maggie asked.

"Three years."

"Anyone since?"

"No."

"Not even a one night stand?"

"Admit it, you fancy him, don't you?"

Maggie looked over at Robert. A female waiter was putting a plate down in front of him. "Certainly not," she said.

"Methinks thou doth protest too much." Pattie laughed.

"He must be a regular here." Maggie looked at Pattie. "I didn't see him order. Yet they knew what he wanted."

"You had your peepers on him all the time. You sly old dog." Pattie laughed. "But you're right, he's a good customer."

"The wages must be good in the policing business if he can afford these prices," Maggie remarked.

"He's very friendly with Cliff, you see."

"That accounts for it then, he obviously gets a discount."

The waiter arrived with the lamb, on gleaming white round plates this time.

Maggie eyed the dish, there didn't seem to be much to this creation either.

Pattie jerked her head in Robert's direction. "Don't look now but he's got company."

Maggie couldn't resist looking.

"That young man is gorgeous, wouldn't you agree?" Pattie said.

Maggie took the opportunity to do the cajoling herself. "Looking for a toy boy are you, Pattie?" she asked.

James Sayder had joined Robert, and after a quick conversation they left together rather hurriedly.

"Something's up," Pattie remarked.

The female waiter who'd noticed Robert's departure removed his plate from the table and headed back to the kitchen with it.

"I wonder what's going on. It has to be something important the way he rushed off," Pattie said.

"Another murder," Maggie jested.

"You could be right."

"Yes, come to think of it, it had to be something important to make him leave in the middle of his beautiful dinner." Maggie got the boot in.

"Oh!" Pattie looked at Maggie with hurt in her eyes. "Don't you like the food here?"

"Of course I do," Maggie lied. "I was only taking the Mickey Finn out of our mutual friend."

Pattie looked relieved.

"I'll hold the front page anyway, and if it turns out to be nothing, I'll just have to make something up, won't I?"

"I never know with you if you're being serious."

"I have a very peculiar sense of humour, but you'll get used to it." Maggie laughed.

"Yes, I suppose I will," Pattie said and then went back to the task of slicing her lamb into neat bite-size pieces.

Maggie had noticed much to her horror that the meat was a bit too pink for her liking and regretted not asking for it to be well done.

"This is delicious," Pattie enthused.

Maggie's mind was working overtime: how on Earth could she possibly eat this sacrificial lamb?

"It is so tender," Patty waved her fork in the air.

Please let someone ring me, Maggie prayed.

CHAPTER 11

Robert and James arrived at Number One Eaton's Grove. "This is totally ridiculous," Robert said.

He had been silent up to then, his mind was on Maggie Lehane much to his own annoyance. He rebuked himself for noticing how attractive she looked sitting there in Cliff's restaurant. White suited her. She should wear that all the time.

"Number One is daft, sir, seeing it's the only house here," James agreed.

"No, I'm talking about the prevention of cruelty to animals people, surely they're the ones that are needed here and not us." Robert forced himself back to the business in hand. He fingered the packet of chewing gum in his pocket. He was still off the cigarettes and finding it extremely hard.

James rang the doorbell and stood back to take his place beside Robert. They hadn't long to wait before an ashen-faced Sally Nolan answered the door.

"Come in." She beckoned them to follow her down the long hall.

She pointed to the oversized couch in the small, cluttered room. "Would you like to sit down?" she asked.

Robert declined the offer when he noticed the couch was full of dog hairs. He threw James a warning look not to take up the invitation either.

"Maybe you would like to tell us what happened, Mrs Nolan," Robert said impatiently.

"It's Miss," Sally corrected. "I'm not married, I'm Miss Nolan."

Robert threw James a look. He just couldn't be bothered with this charade. "James will ask you a few questions," he said.

"Could you tell us what happened, Miss Nolan?"

"I came back from the shops and found her on the doorstep."

"What's her name?"

"Bonnie," Sally answered. She proceeded to take a tissue from an unopened box on the coffee table. As she struggled to open it, her hands were visibly shaking.

James jumped to her aid. He opened the box and handed her some tissues.

"The blood…" She struggled to compose herself and blew her nose.

James handed her some fresh tissues. "Take your time," he said.

Robert couldn't help but admire James; so wise for one so young, he mused.

"So, what did you do then?" James encouraged her to go on.

"I called the vet, you fool."

James didn't seem to mind being spoken to in that manner. "Good thinking," he said.

"He came straightaway, but there was nothing he could do. He said that Bonnie's tongue had been cut out, and her eyes too; and the ears. Who could do such a thing to a dumb animal?"

Robert almost laughed at the woman's choice of the word dumb. The brave Bonnie would certainly be dumb after a tongue removal.

It was as if Sally Nolan had read his mind given the way she suddenly diverted her attention to him. Her eyes were like laser beams, he'd be lucky if there weren't two holes bored into his forehead.

She scowled at him, obviously aware of his lack of compassion. If he didn't get out of here soon, he'd crack up.

"Did you notice anything unusual?" James continued with the questioning. On seeing her blank expression, he expounded, "Someone hanging around, young boys for instance."

"No, there was nobody around. Not one soul," Sally said. "This is the quietest part of town, you could be dead out here and nobody would know," she added.

"Right," Robert said, sharply intimating the interview was over. He had had enough, and he was adamant it was a total waste of time continuing with this indulgence.

"As true as God I'm going to be next." Sally wasn't finished.

"Don't be silly," Robert retorted.

"It's a message, I tell you."

"Don't upset yourself, Miss Nolan." James was far more accommodating. "It's just the work of a few yobs that have no regard for man or beast."

"It's a message, I'm telling you." Sally scowled. There was no way she was going to accept that assumption.

"Do you have a suspect in mind?" Robert decided to humour her so that the whole thing could come to a swift end. His head was reeling from the smell in the room. That was the downside of animals, they always stank the place out no matter how much you groomed them. The nature of the beast, so to speak.

James wasn't giving up just yet though. He seemed intrigued with Sally's suspicions. "So, you think someone has it in for you?" he asked.

Robert muttered under his breath. Why was James allowing himself to get sucked into this fairy tale?

"Do you think there might be someone who might have a grudge against you, Miss Nolan? I'm not suggesting that you would upset anyone to that extent, but sometimes people do get the strangest of ideas, don't they?" James reasoned.

"I'm sure you have nothing to worry about, Miss Nolan," Robert said dismissively and headed for the door.

"Try not to worry." James smiled sympathetically at the distraught woman, and then made to follow Robert out of the room.

"We'll see ourselves out," Robert called over his shoulder.

Once outside, Robert opened a packet of chewing gum and put a piece in his mouth.

"You off the ciggies, sir?" James asked.

Robert ignored the question and remarked, "Like you said, James, it's yobs that did this. Getting their kicks out of mindless behaviour, it happens, you know."

James shook his head. "I only said that for her benefit, it's far more sinister than that. I'm sure there's something nasty going on, she thinks so too, didn't you see how wound up she was?"

"Yes, and did you notice the picture she had hanging up over the mantelpiece?"

"The Queen," James said. "I saw that."

"Maybe it's the IRA that's after her," Robert said with a laugh.

James didn't appreciate the joke.

"If she suspects she has an enemy, why doesn't she name him, give us something concrete to work on?" Robert said.

"But that's the thing you see, she could have got up someone's nose and not known it."

"There are people who get up my nose but I don't go around killing their dogs," Robert retorted. "I'd like to, but I don't."

"But that's you, sir, you're in control of your faculties, but the fact remains that there are psychopaths out there. Lunatics who go right over the edge to pay people back for wrongs done to them, whether real or imaginary."

"No, I'm sticking with the yobs theory. They were probably drugged up to their eyeballs and off their heads with drink. Let's hope they're going to stop at that though, we don't want a rampage of animal sacrifice here in Magnerstown, on top of a murder," Robert said.

"We should have given her a little more time," James suggested carefully. He didn't want to sound as if he was questioning Robert's dismissal of the situation. He thought Robert was wrong, but would never in a million years say it to his face.

"I'm going to be next, she said, if you ask me that's what's wrong there. Paranoia of the highest order, and I bet her favourite reading matter is Agatha Christie's novels. You know the ones where there's ten people getting bumped off one by one." Robert walked on ahead of James.

"But the killing of the dog, sir, that's not a figment of her imagination, is it?"

Robert turned around briefly. "Nobody is going to kill her, right? Do you get it, she is not going to be killed, now let's leave it at that," he said.

"Whatever you say, sir," James said. He dutifully followed on behind. He would have liked to have talked more to Sally Nolan, drawn her out. Maybe he could slip back sometime today and see her on his own. He brightened at the thought, but Robert was the boss in this instance, and if he found out he'd gone behind his back he'd be extremely annoyed. He would just have to leave well enough alone, because he didn't want to get on the wrong side of the man, although it might be too late for that. He couldn't help feeling he was already on the wrong side, for some reason he couldn't quite fathom.

CHAPTER 12

Greg Joubert emptied the contents of the plastic supermarket carrier bag onto the campervan worktop. He had to buy perishable food on a daily basis because there wasn't much room in the tiny fridge. Tonight he was having marinated pork chops for supper. He'd become adept at using the right combination of ingredients for meals for one, so there was seldom much leftover.

Nonetheless, he was now expert at getting rid of rubbish. Leftover bread, the birds happily pecked away at. Potato and vegetable peelings, he'd pile into a carrier bag and take to the rubbish bin which was for the use of walkers in the woods. The bin was usually piled high with empty cans and plastic bottles, but he always managed to squeeze his throwaways in under them. The bin was emptied regularly by the FAS people. Foras Áiseanna Saothair to give their full title. The English translation was, The Labour Facilities Foundation, a state agency who provided training for unemployed people. He'd found all that out from one of the fellows who'd started to become a bit too friendly, until he knocked him back into place, but apart from that he was a likeable sort, and handy for information.

The FAS workmen were putting down pebbles on the paths which wound and twisted their way through the woods. This was being done because after a bout of heavy rain the natural paths turned into mud baths, and were impassable. A few of the locals had set up a committee to promote the area as a tourist attraction. They hoped the project would bring economic benefits to the small businesses and bed-and-breakfast outfits in the area. According to the information he'd been given by his trusty FAS friend, the committee had lobbied the government to plough some money into the idea. That approach brought good results as the men in suits agreed it was a great concept. They approved a scheme which would pay for both the materials and the workers, and that had the knock-on effect of everyone being happy.

They could do with some of those FAS boys to work on the hiking trails on Table Mountain at home. Greg smiled wryly.

He had never forgotten the magic of his first visit to the mountain. The Jouberts had taken him there, and it was all so spectacular to a young boy. With so many things to explore, he'd been overwhelmed and wished he could live there forever.

They were happy then, him and the Jouberts, before he got to the stage when he could see the chinks in their armour. They had too much money for a start; they thought they could buy anything, and they were right in that respect. They were able to buy a child, him, as it happened, with their dirty money.

He didn't like the way they made their profits in that pet food factory of theirs, thanks to the slave labour they employed. He had never liked the idea of that practice. They knew how he felt about their mistreatment of the workers; they didn't even supply them with masks or protective clothing. Health and safety was a dirty word, anyone who mentioned it got the boot. He told them often enough what he thought of the whole issue. They always laughed at him and told him he wasn't living in the real world.

Those poor black people were willing to work the round of the clock and take what they got. They never complained because they knew there were others waiting on the sidelines, ready to step into their shoes.

It came as no surprise to the Jouberts when Greg announced that he would not be having anything to do with the factory. He wanted to go his own way, and no one would persuade him otherwise.

After doing his stint in college he drifted in and out of jobs, mostly because they didn't give him any satisfaction or feeling of self-worth. He was determined not to give in to his keepers and end up in their dog fodder labour camp. Not even the easy job that they'd promised could entice him.

As he had no desire for gracious living, and his needs were small, he managed to survive without their financial input.

He sometimes wondered if he'd been a gypsy in a former life, wandering around from town to town in a caravan, seeing how he seemed to enjoy that kind of living. It was the freedom of not being tied down that gave him so much pleasure. He firmly believed he was a nomad reborn.

Greg turned his attention to peeling his three red rooster potatoes and putting them on to boil. He liked to use fresh produce whenever he could. True, they had trays of readymade mash in the supermarket, which would save him all this trouble, but it was too stodgy and didn't at all taste like real potatoes to him. A white blob of goo is what it looked like, and yet people bought the muck. He was surprised that there was a market for it, but still, there was no accounting for taste.

He poured some extra virgin olive oil into the large frying pan and waited for it to heat up to just the right temperature before adding the marinated chops. They sizzled as they touched the pan, and instantly the aroma from the herbs in the marinade pinched his nostrils. There was nothing quite like the smell of good food to give you an appetite. Quickly, he chopped the onion and added it to the pan. When he was satisfied with his culinary task he tipped the contents into a casserole dish and put it into the oven to keep it warm. He opened the tin of sweet corn which was flavoured with peppers, emptied the contents into a small saucepan and placed it onto the ring vacated by the frying pan. Sure, it was cramped in here, and everything he did had to be planned and carried out with precision, but he wouldn't swap it for anything, not even the luxury of a hotel suite. He liked his privacy and the effort was worth it, far better than staying in a bed and breakfast with your comings and goings being noted by some nosey landlady.

He liked it here in Dunem Woods. Night-time was his favourite because it reminded him of home. The quietness disturbed only by the sound of a sudden movement or cry of a bird, or the barking of a dog in the distance. It was amazing the way sounds carried so far in the middle of the night. On the other hand, there were a few squirrels who didn't keep their distance. The little buggers had no qualms about making their presence known. He disliked the fact that they were the dreaded grey ones, and hated that they were fast outnumbering the red species. It was the same back home. They were quite cheeky, the little ones here in Dunem Woods, they seemed to delight in scampering across the roof of the van, but even though he complained about them, deep down he liked the company.

After he had eaten, Greg went to his mini fridge for the luxury he'd allowed himself for the day, a lemon cheesecake. This was the one convenience food that he had no problem with. He glanced at the foil wrapped package tucked away in the back of the fridge and smiled. That part of the plan would be coming into play pretty soon. He made a mental note of his agenda for the coming few hours; he'd better get a move on, he told himself. Firstly, he had to get to the internet cafe and do the stuff on his list, and after that there was a delivery to make.

On completion of those tasks he would call to the bottle store and get a few beers as a reward.

He had a master plan, and up to now everything was going quite well. He was real proud of himself for that, and it didn't harm a person to grant themselves a little praise now and then.

He smiled as he sat down to eat his dessert. He was quite certain it would taste as good as it looked, despite the fact he hadn't made it with his own very capable hands.

CHAPTER 13

Maggie arrived back to Forge Cottage feeling bloated and at least a stone heavier. The banana fritters and ice-cream she'd had to round off the disastrous meal at Cliff's was coming back to haunt her. She had no Alka-Seltzer in the house, because she had used the last two a few nights earlier after a disastrous concoction she had eaten. The blame for that lay solely with herself: she had thrown spices and nuts and the dregs of a bottle of red into the mix like she was on MasterChef. She'd have been done for attempted murder if she'd served it up to someone other than herself.

It was too late now to get the tablets in any of the shops, and Magnerstown didn't have the luxury of an all-night chemist.

After parking up her car, she decided to go for a short walk, which she was sure would bring some kind of relief. In any case she had been falling down on her exercise regime lately, so a half an hour of a left-right, left-right march wouldn't go astray. Much as she hated to admit it, all the good intentions she'd had for a healthier lifestyle in all aspects of her life were slipping away by degrees, so she'd have to rectify that immediately or else she'd end up in hospital. Her stomach was playing up and that was a warning sign she'd be stupid to ignore. The body knows.

Ten minutes into the walk she started to feel better, the fresh air was helping too, and the peace and quiet was really enjoyable. Everyone must be in bed, she reasoned, until the sound of an approaching car broke the spell.

As the car drew level it slowed, which didn't freak her out in the slightest. She didn't feel she had anything to fear from the situation, it was a different scenario now since leaving city life behind. This was a safe little town; true, there had been a murder, but that was another issue altogether.

She could see the driver quite plainly but couldn't make out the passenger at all.

There was a wave of a hand before the car gathered speed and drove off into the night.

It was James Sayder, there was no mistaking that ponytail, and obviously his passenger was the wonderful detective inspector. There was something about Robert Carroll that annoyed her.

Why did his fiancée leave him? she wondered. Pattie was convinced an affair was to blame, which meant that his woman must have been unhappy if someone else turned her head. If they were married you could put it down to the seven-year itch or something of that nature.

Did the breakup upset Mister Robert, or was he glad of the way out? He wasn't really relationship material, she figured, and laughed at the irony of her thoughts. She couldn't talk, seeing she herself hadn't much luck in that department either, though that could be down to the fact that she had the unhappy knack of always choosing the wrong man. Things would appear to get off to a great start, but sooner or later either she or the gentleman in question would call a halt when the novelty wore off. The ones who were dead keen would vanish too, when they worked out she wouldn't give a commitment. 'There's no point in us wasting time,' one such hapless creature had told her after only six months dating, and how right he was. Wasting time should be a grievous sin, punishable by fire and brimstone in the next life.

Was she right at all to keep blaming her parents' miserable relationship for her own shortcomings with men? She remembered the constant rows between them, and always because of some woman or other.

Maggie could never rationalize why her father couldn't keep his paws off other women when he had a beautiful wife at home. She was highly intelligent too, but it wasn't enough for him. Serial adulterer was the name for people of his ilk.

On that thought, she turned and headed back to Forge Cottage. She really loved this place, she realized, and a huge feeling of contentment swept over her.

She bent down, removed the key from under the mat and returned it to its hiding place after opening the front door.

Stepping into the hall she spotted a big brown envelope. Was it possible the mysterious furnisher of news had made contact again?

She made her way to the kitchen, poured herself half a glass of red wine, and then carefully opened the envelope.

Her hunch was right, it was from her contact. He had signed the note like before with the words 'Concerned Citizen.'

There was a photo of a dead dog, and a note revealing the name and address of the misfortunate owner. Finally, the circumstance of the animal's untimely death was spelt out in detail.

What a cruel thing to do. Maggie shook her head at the thought of such a sickening act.

She'd get Joey Tyrell to visit Miss Nolan tomorrow at some stage. This had all the makings of a good human-interest story, and where better to put it but on the front page?

She was grateful to the 'Concerned Citizen,' whoever he was. It was then the thought struck her, it could be a woman and not a man as she had presumed; but what did it matter? He or she was providing a lot of good material for *The Crier* and that was the reason it was selling like hot cakes.

Outside, the hooded figure standing under the cherry tree sighed with relief. That was a close shave.

Quietly, like a thief in the night, the figure briskly moved out onto the road, and blended into the darkness.

CHAPTER 14

Robert Carroll made himself a cup of tea, and after two mouthfuls he promptly emptied the rest into the sink and watched it disappear down the plug hole. He turned on the cold-water tap and allowed it to flow long enough to remove every trace of the liquid from the so-called stainless-steel sink. Tea stains became troublesome if not dealt with instantly. He wasn't obsessively house-proud; it was just that he liked to save himself the bother of scrubbing and rubbing around the house. 'Clean as you go' had become his motto, after he had seen the slogan above the sink in the local delicatessen. He often called there for a takeaway sandwich when he felt too tired to even contemplate rustling up something to eat at home.

A proper drink was what he needed right now. He lost no time in pouring out a very large one.

He turned on his CD player, and as the music of the French Classical composer Eric Satie broke the silence, he settled himself down on the couch. He especially liked *Gnossienne No.1*.

Annie used to play that particular piece on the piano when they'd lived in France. They were happy then. Annie was the one who had introduced him to all things French, even the Hennessey's Cognac that he'd come to love so much. He smiled remembering how she told him the history of the drink. It was distilled from white wine, and named after the French town where it was produced. She had also filled him in on Satie. He was an eccentric gentleman who was his own man when it came to music, but his private life was bizarre. Satie had once purchased twelve grey velvet suits, which he wore one at a time until they wore out. On his death, six suits were discovered unused in his wardrobe. There were one hundred umbrellas in his apartment, yet another example of his strange behaviour.

Yes indeed, he learned a lot from Annie, and she helped him with the language, to give her her due.

He sighed heavily, he felt so jaded lately and going to the doctor was not an option because he knew what the results would be. He'd be told he was suffering from depression like before. He'd taken Cipramil then, the so-called wonder drug for depression. It was supposed to breathe new life and energy into you, make you happy, but all it had done for him was wind him down. He was so laid back while taking the medication that he was practically docile, and he did not like being in that kind of state.

His thoughts turned to the situation in hand, a murder of all things, and in this sleepy town too. It was ironic seeing as he'd moved back here in the first place to get away from that kind of mayhem. A quiet life was what he'd come to desire, now that he was at the halfway mark in life. He was a proper mess, no doubt about that, and in the wrong profession, to make matters worse.

His father had been high up in the ranks, and it was expected that his only son should become a copper too, so without question Robert fell into it, and went through the motions on a daily basis.

Robert finished the cognac in two gulps and got up to refill his glass. This time he filled the glass right to the top;

it would save him the bother of getting up every five minutes.

His father was policing in heaven now, he smiled wryly, and not here to keep him in check. So, there was no need to keep pressuring himself, and no point in keeping up the pretence by continuing in a job that he hated. But what could he do with himself at this point of his life? Was it too late to start a new career considering he'd be fifty in a few years' time? He didn't know the answers to these questions; he'd never actually allowed himself to think of alternatives because that would demand too much effort. Change in itself would be a huge upheaval, and he was, as he often admitted to himself, a lazy spineless git.

He could go abroad again and see how things would go there, that was if he could motivate himself. There was nothing to stop him, was there? He had no ties to bind him, he was his own man so to speak.

His thoughts returned to Annie and the night he caught her with Cliff. The way out of the relationship was presented to him there and then on a plate. He had a right good excuse for throwing the blame for the breakup at her door.

She'd defended herself well enough, and a good show she made of it too. Did she think he was daft enough to believe her fairy story? She said that Cliff had been harassing her for some time, and on that fateful night Cliff had been drunk and insistent, and all she was doing was humouring him until he tired of his fumbling.

She'd pleaded with Robert to believe her, but he made it plain he could never trust her again.

He saw what he saw, he insisted. Did she think he was such a total idiot that he didn't recognize what was going on under his nose?

"You saw what you wanted to see," Annie had argued.

Was she right about that? Did he see what he wanted to see only because the relationship had gone stale for him? In hindsight, there was never any real spark there for him. Annie had picked him up like a lost puppy and the whole thing just muddled along like everything else in his life. Hour after hour, day after day, year after year, Jesus it was all one long tedious journey.

Robert placed the glass on the couch beside him. It was a two-seater that Annie picked out. She said it was more intimate. He'd been meaning to get rid of it because he couldn't lie down on it and stretch his legs out.

Had he been unfair to Annie? He'd allowed her to uproot herself and come to Magnerstown, his so-called hometown. Hometown was a bit of an exaggeration. He had gone away to college at the age of eighteen, and when he returned to take up a job in policing like his father had wanted him to, he felt stifled in the provincial town.

Against his father's wishes he left the job and the town behind, ironically on his birthday, when he was just twenty-four.

He spent the next twenty years in France, and what had he to show for it all? Nothing, that's what it had all amounted to in the end. One great fat heap of nothing.

He had drifted from place to place in France searching; for what exactly? Would he even know what it was if he found it?

Was he drunk the night he agreed with Annie that returning to his roots could be a new start for both of them?

While they settled into Magnerstown as a couple he had come to realize that he'd lost all contacts with the people he knew from the past. Friends were very thin on the ground, and as for the town itself, it was nothing like the one he'd left behind. In a matter of two decades it had changed into some other kind of place. Once again he was a stranger, trying to fit in.

Was anything ever going to go right for him? He sighed as he placed the empty glass on the coffee table.

Here he was at this point of his life, all alone, hitting fifty, which was exactly the age his father had been when he died unexpectedly.

Was he going to face an early grave too? Did he even care at this point? He could go to the graveyard this minute with a shovel and bury himself.

To hell with it all. He moaned softly as he laid back on the couch and closed his eyes.

Post-mortems on the past only drained him and filled him with regret, and thoughts of the future filled him with fear, so he was better living in the now, bad as it was.

Five minutes later, he was fast asleep.

CHAPTER 15

Joey Tyrell arrived at Number One Eaton's Grove feeling full of the joys of spring. It was great to be working again. The minute he laid eyes on Miss Sally Nolan he took an instant dislike to her, and he didn't know why.

"I don't really want to attract attention to myself," she told Joey after hearing his introduction and intentions for an article on her situation.

"You may save other unfortunate animals from the same fate," Joey reasoned. "Someone somewhere knows the individuals who killed your dog, and your story in the paper could be the prompt they need to pass on this vital information to the boys in blue."

"I'm not sure."

"You would be doing a really great service to the community, you know?"

She seemed to soften after digesting this point of view.

"Right, come in before I change my mind," she said.

Seating himself at the kitchen table, Joey took out his notebook and began writing with the thought running through his head that he knew this woman from somewhere in the past. Even though Magnerstown was a small place you didn't necessarily know everyone in it. There were people leaving and people coming to the area all the time; plus, not everyone moved in the same circles. This woman on the other hand was so familiar, and yet he couldn't place her. What he did know was that he did not like her.

"Someone has it in for me," Sally announced.

This is going to be interesting, Joey thought, feeling inwardly pleased.

"How could anyone want to harm you? You're such a respectable kind of person." Joey congratulated himself on how genuine he was sounding. "I couldn't imagine you doing anyone a bad turn." He was on a roll now.

"That maybe so, but there's a lot of crazy people around nowadays," Sally retorted.

Even her voice was familiar: that upper crust twang was so irritating; who the hell was she? Joey's curiosity was getting the better of him. There was only one thing for it, he'd have to ask her straight out.

"Have you always lived here in Magnerstown, Miss Nolan?" he ventured.

"Quite a good few years, yes," she said cagily.

"Did you work in the town? Mind if I ask you what your profession was?"

"I was a secretary," she replied. "My first job was here in this very house."

"Oh, who was your boss?" Joey asked.

"I'd rather not say, if you don't mind."

"I take it you're retired," Joey said carefully. Some women were very touchy about their age.

"I retired early," Sally snapped. She was annoyed that he should think she was older than she was.

Christ, but this is one jumpy woman, Joey thought.

"When the job here came to an end, I was employed by Carter Jones & Sons Solicitors," she announced. "I was Mr Jones senior's secretary until he died. It was then that I retired. His son took over, and in my opinion he's not a patch on his father."

That's it, Joey remembered now, his mind racing back to a past experience.

It was ten years ago and he was going through a silly phase at the time, drinking too much and smoking hash, and of course he had the misfortune to come to the attention of the good old boys in blue.

Mates doing far worse than him didn't get caught, but he wasn't that lucky. He'd found himself before that mouldy old dinosaur Judge Mangan who fined him a hundred pounds, which was quite a hefty fine in those days, for being in possession of an illegal substance. He'd had to pay the fine off at a fiver a week or else go to gaol, and here he was now, face to face with the woman who dealt with him at the solicitor's.

She used to treat him like dirt; he remembered it so well. You'd think he was a leper the way she used to throw the receipt at him, and what was his crime? Having one flipping joint on him.

How ironic that he should be interviewing this old bag now. He was confident enough that she hadn't recognized him, after all he hadn't told her his name, only that he was from *The Crier*.

With regard to his looks, he had improved from the scruffy long-haired bearded hippy that he was then, to a much tidier version.

"You were saying someone has it in for you," Joey prompted.

"They killed my dog and I'm going to be next," Sally replied.

"No, not at all, why would someone want to do that?"

It killed him to say it but Joey knew he had to keep up the pretence. She deserved the kick up the arse she got over her flea-bitten dog and more besides, as far as he was concerned.

Joey noticed with surprise that she was studying his name badge.

"Joey Tyrell," she read aloud.

He'd forgotten he was advertising that vital bit of information.

"That's a familiar name."

Joey tried to distract her by changing the subject.

She ignored him and repeated his name again. Then, her expression changed.

"I know who you are now," she said harshly. "You're that young delinquent who was selling drugs."

"I was not selling drugs."

"You should have got gaol," she scowled. "You're the scum of the Earth you and your lot."

Joey was fuming. The cheek of this woman making unfair assumptions, when she knew nothing at all about his private circumstances, for fuck sake.

It angered him now, thinking back to how that ignorant ill-informed judge decided he was going to make an example out of him.

'Let this be a lesson to others.' Joey could still hear the judge's superior voice ringing out all over the courtroom, like he was judging the crime of the century. Oh how sweet it was that the past came back to haunt the superior old fucker. Wonderful to know he had ended up with his superior old throat ripped open. Yes, it was a fitting end for him; Joey felt a warm glow inside.

"Get out of my house," Sally Nolan ordered venomously. "And I've a good mind to ring that boss of yours and have you sacked," she added.

Joey rose to his feet. Right in the mush he'd give it to her, because she was asking for it.

"You stupid fucking old bag," he spat at her, his face only an inch away from hers. "Yeah, you're right. Your dog was a message. You're going to die next, you tight-arsed old cow."

* * *

76

Greg Joubert left the internet cafe pulling his hood up when he noted it was starting to rain. He tucked the brown envelope inside his fleece as he didn't want it getting wet.

He was lucky to have access to the internet cafe after opening hours. He'd struck up an acquaintance with the owner, a foreign fellow who didn't ask questions. All he was interested in was the generous sum of money that Greg gave him for the private use of the place. Tonight, Greg had been printing off several images from his camera, and they were the kind of pictures you wouldn't want someone looking over your shoulder at.

He didn't see the hairy fellow coming and almost knocked him down.

"Howzit," Greg tapped the fellow on the shoulder apologetically.

"Me head's fried, is the internet cafe still open?" Joey was out of breath.

"No, but he's still inside."

"Thanks." Joey tapped on the window.

Greg moved off as soon as the door was opened.

CHAPTER 16

Frankie Bergin had to stand on his tiptoes to reach the doorbell of Number One Eaton's Grove.

He was small for his age and well aware of it, because everyone in his class towered above him. However, being small had some distinct advantages. People were inclined to feel sorry for him, so he got away with most things.

Surveying the affluence of the place, he told the bundle in his arms, "You'll be well looked after here 'cos you'd have to be a rich person to own a place like this."

He waited for what he considered a respectable period, but the door wasn't answered.

He presumed the parked car belonged to the owner, so she had to be in. With that in mind he decided to reach up again and give the bell another go.

The puppy which was snugly wrapped in one of his old jumpers whimpered.

Frankie could hear the bell ringing, so that confirmed it wasn't out of order, like the one at home. Not that there was anything terribly wrong with their bell, the battery was dead. His mother kept repeating her promise to buy a new battery on her next visit to the shops, and yet on the few occasions that he reminded her when she was making out her shopping list, she'd say, 'I'm a little short today, next time I'll get it, Frankie.'

She smoked a whole packet of cigarettes every day, and the way Frankie saw it, she'd make a huge saving if she gave them up.

They were bad for your health. His father was proof enough of that, because he had died from lung cancer last year, but still his mother hadn't got the message. But then he supposed, when all was said and done, he preferred it that smoking was all she did. It could be worse. She could be going out every Saturday night to the pub, and bringing every Tom, Dick or Harry back home like Jimmy McGrath's mother did. The boys in school goaded Jimmy about his mother. They called her the town bike, which was really hurtful to Jimmy.

His thoughts returned to the matter in hand, there was still no reply and he was anxious to get the matter sorted out today.

The story about the murdered dog was big news in school. It had been on the front page of the local paper and all. They were appealing for anyone with information to come forward before any other dog met with the same fate. Their own dog Daisy had not been allowed out on her own just in case she had the bad luck to bump into those vicious killers. He knew how sad he'd be if anything were to happen to Daisy, so he could well understand how the woman living here must be feeling at the loss of her pet. His big idea came to him while he was daydreaming in history class. Maybe the grieving woman might accept the present of a puppy.

He didn't want any money for it in return. The fact that the animal would be saved from certain death would be reward enough.

Daisy had produced four puppies this time, and thankfully the three who were boys had been given away to good homes, but the little one in his arms hadn't been so lucky. No one ever seemed to want girl dogs. She would end up disappearing overnight like the others before her, and he knew in his heart of hearts that they had all ended up in the bottom of the green river.

A simple operation would stop Daisy producing any more pups, but it would cost eighty euros, and he didn't dare suggest it at home. He knew that was the price the vets charged because one of the boys in his class had been boasting in the schoolyard that they had had their pet done. The boy had also gone into detail about how the operation was performed, and how the poor animal had staggered around the place still under the influence of the anaesthetic when it got home. It was at this point of the re-enactment that Frankie sloped away. That part of it was not nice, but the end result was worth it, he supposed.

It was now clear to Frankie that the owner of Number One Eaton's Grove was not going to answer the door, more than likely because she thought he was a ticket seller or something to that effect.

He noticed there was a side entrance to the house and even better still, the gate was open.

He made his way up the garden path before coming face to face with a massive window which nearly took up the whole wall, and that was a good thing because he'd be able to see straight in.

He pressed his face up against the window and took in the scene. It was a kitchen, no doubt about that. He could just about make out a figure sitting at the table.

He tapped on the window to attract attention, but that got no results at all. Could she be a little hard of hearing? Lots of old people suffered with that complaint. His grandfather was completely deaf before he died. Although his mother often said it was selective deafness, whatever that meant.

Frankie focused again on the woman. She looked like she was asleep which prompted him to knock as loud as he could, but that didn't work either. There was no stir out of her at all.

Was she dead? he wondered. Had she suffered a heart attack or something?

She was a pensioner the newspaper said, and he knew a lot of old people had heart problems. Again, he pressed his face against the window and willed her to look in his direction.

This time he saw something new. There was a lot of red stuff on the woman's white blouse. He continued to stare long and hard. The red stuff was blood, he could see that now, and it was obvious to him that this person was very much dead.

It was time for action. Frankie stepped back.

What could he do, though? Go to the newspaper people and tell them.

Would they give him a reward? If he got eighty euros he could pay for Daisy to go to the vet.

* * *

Maggie had been disappointed when Joey Tyrell told her he had not been successful with Sally Nolan, but the pictures she was now staring at caused the hairs on the back of her neck to rise.

The pictures of Sally Nolan were stark and horrible, what a terrible way to die. Maggie looked at the brown envelope they'd arrived in and shook her head. There had been no news of Sally's body being discovered, unless of course the police were keeping it under wraps, which she doubted was the case. If she gave them this information they would pull Joey in, seeing he could have been the last one to see her before the murderer arrived. Someone was bound to have seen him. Was Joey in fact... No, she wouldn't allow herself to go there, no way was Joey the murderer.

Robert Carroll would think that way too, knowing him; he would want a scapegoat, and anyone would do. She would not offer Joey Tyrell's head on a plate to Mr 'Salome' Carroll.

Frankie looked up at the name over the door. *The Crier.*

He would have to think about this.

CHAPTER 17

James Sayder pushed *The Crier* across the table to Robert. "Our Miss Lehane has done it again," he said.

"Another coffee please," Robert called to the barman.

He was fuming over having to have coffee in the pub because the vending machine in the station was out of order. His suggestion to buy a few electric kettles to tide them over was deemed out of the question because of the new rules.

"Health and safety, my arse," Robert said aloud.

James looked at him quizzically.

"Just thinking about something." Robert picked up the paper and scanned the front page.

"Animal sacrifices in Magnerstown," Robert read out the headline.

"Let's hope it doesn't give ideas to cranks," James interjected.

"We'll have some lunatic jumping on the bandwagon now," Robert said.

James laughed softly.

Robert turned his attention to the barman who seemed to be deep in conversation with a punter.

"Coffee, here," Robert shouted.

The barman nodded in acknowledgement.

"Who's that fellow?" James asked.

"Benny something-or-other, why?"

"No, not the barman, the fellow supping the pint I mean."

"Toby Jackson; don't you remember? He's the man who discovered the judge's body. Well, it was him and half the town to be absolutely correct about it," Robert said.

"We never spoke to him," James said.

"Why would we want to?" Robert frowned.

"One coffee," the barman said pointedly as he laid the mug and saucer down on the table.

"Thanks," Robert said.

The barman turned his attention to the newspaper in Robert's hand. "We'll have a witches' coven in the woods next, with goats laid out on altars of stone having their throats cut."

Robert didn't even bother to reply.

James pushed the milk and sugar towards Robert.

"All they want to do is serve drink," Robert muttered as soon as Benny was out of earshot.

"It's easier than boiling a kettle," James joked.

"There's more profit in coffee than drink I'd imagine. You can buy a jar of coffee for the prices they're charging for one miserly cup. Still, what can you do?" Robert sighed.

"You still off the weed?" James asked.

"Yes," Robert answered sharply.

"Well done."

"Did you ever smoke?"

"You could say I started and stopped all in the space of five minutes," James laughed. "It was a case of a few drags behind the bike shed in school, I was being egged on, you see."

"The infamous old peer-pressure job." Robert put the mug to his lips.

"I got uncontrollably sick all over one of the lads. I never dared to smoke again, nor was I asked."

"That would do it alright." Robert pulled a face and put the mug back on the saucer. "That is the most disgusting piss I have ever tasted, it's even worse than the first lot he made." Robert shot a look at the barman. "He didn't even bother to re-boil the kettle. It's fucking lukewarm, like him. And what's the saucer about?"

"Saves on coasters." James grinned.

Robert pushed the coffee away. "They get them for nothing," he said.

"This photo of the dog," James pointed to the paper. "I wonder where our esteemed editor got it from."

"The vet probably," Robert said.

"Do you think so?"

"You could check it out," Robert remarked. He deliberately put the emphasis on the 'you'.

"I can't help wondering where Miss Lehane is getting her information from," James remarked.

"Maybe she's got a team of bloodhounds for reporters," Robert said. "Let's hope they don't end up as sacrifices, like poor old Bonnie." Robert looked at James expecting him to react to his attempt at being funny. James appeared to be deep in thought.

"Do you get the whiff of cigarette smoke?" Robert raised his voice to get attention.

"That'll be the upholstery, sir."

"Maybe Benny might clean it with his lukewarm water." Robert threw a look in the direction of the bar.

James had hit on something with the upholstery thing, Robert thought. The love seat at home could trigger a nicotine relapse if he didn't do something about it. This was a great excuse for shafting it.

"Whoever is leaking information to *The Crier* is doing it for the money. Either someone on the outside, or someone on the inside."

"The inside?"

"Someone wanting to keep themselves in a job," James answered.

"There'd be no harm in you following up on your hunches," Robert stated. He did admire James's astuteness, even if it was with some reluctance.

All heads turned in the direction of the door as a red-faced Sergeant Hickey came running in.

"Sally Nolan has been found dead in her house," he blurted out at the top of his voice.

CHAPTER 18

When Robert arrived at the morgue, he was surprised to find that James Sayder was not there.

Dr Morris removed his purple plastic gloves and deposited them in the large silver bin before addressing Robert.

Robert could never understand how pathologists could do the job. He himself would not do it, not for a million euro a week even.

"Her main artery was severed," Dr Morris said. "The interesting thing–" The doctor stopped abruptly when the door burst open, and an out-of-breath James Sayder came rushing in.

"Sorry I'm late," James said.

"Her main artery was severed." Robert filled James in before gesturing to the doctor to continue with his report.

"The interesting thing is her throat was slashed in exactly the same way as Judge Mangan's, except her hands weren't mutilated like his," Dr Morris revealed. "I'd lay my career on the line and say the two killings were done by the same person."

"We have a serial killer in Magnerstown." James didn't bother hiding his excitement.

Dr Morris removed his disposable apron and binned it. "You'll never guess what I found in her mouth?"

"What?" Robert asked.

"The tongue, eyes and ears of a dog," the doctor replied.

"Doesn't it remind you of the three wise monkeys?" James remarked.

"See no evil, hear no evil," Doctor Morris said.

Robert shook his head. "There's a very sick person out there," he said.

"There is evidence that she was in the early stages of choking, but of course it was the knifing that killed her," Doctor Morris said.

"Some death," James said.

"Wasn't it just?" Robert agreed.

"The vet confirmed that the items in her mouth were likely those of her pet dog."

James gave Robert a sideways look. "She was right about the killing of her dog being a message."

"Yeah, I stand corrected," Robert sighed.

"She had been dead for three days," Dr Morris revealed.

"You're joking," Robert said.

"And nobody missed her." James was surprised that a thing like that could be possible in a small town.

"If that young boy hadn't found her, she'd probably still be up there. I hope he is going to get some sort of a reward, must have been a horrible thing for one so young to see," Dr Morris remarked.

"I'm sure something can be arranged. I'll see to it," Robert said.

"You might be interested in this. I had a phone call from an old acquaintance the other night. I say acquaintance but he wasn't really. I only met him once or twice at medical conventions, but the funny thing is I never met him when he was actually working in this area," the doctor said.

"You mean here in the town?" asked Robert.

"Just on the verge of town to be precise, anyway the upshot is this man, Dr Curtin, is interested in the case because he had some kind of dealings with the judge, you see. Wait a minute, did he say they were friends? My memory is not what it used to be."

"We can all relate to that," Robert said.

"However, we talked about the way the judge met his Waterloo. Well, the thing he picked up on was the way the judge's hands were cut," Dr Morris said.

Robert could feel a litany of psychological jargon was on the way.

"Well, according to Dr Curtin who happens to be a psychiatrist by the way–"

"Thought so," Robert interjected.

"That kind of injury is usually inflicted by an offspring, patricide it's called."

"Oh, for God's sake," Robert scoffed.

"Would you expound on that?" asked James, who was clearly more open to the idea.

"Case studies of adult children who kill a parent or both parents in some cases have shown that a frenzied attack is normally administered as a form of a punishment. In other words, the parent could have been an abuser or a control freak."

"In the case of both parents, the second one could get it for standing idly by," James offered.

"Exactly," Dr Morris smiled. "You know about this kind of thing then."

"Came up in my studies," James replied.

"But Judge Mangan didn't have any children, did he?" Robert argued. "He wasn't even married."

"Not that you have to be married to have children," Dr Morris said.

"It wouldn't be any harm to meet this contact of yours, Dr Morris, would it?" James said.

"I can't help you there," the doctor replied. "He retired when the place where he worked closed down. He went off to live in some obscure residence up a mountain according to the person who happened to be with me when I got the phone call."

Noting the smile on the doctor's face Robert presumed the person who happened to be with him was female.

"Have you a number for him?" James asked.

"As I said, he phoned me, but unfortunately the number was withheld."

"There has to be a connection between these two murders," said James, addressing Robert.

"That's for you two to find out." Dr Morris's expression indicated the meeting was over.

The two men turned and headed for the door, only to be stopped in their tracks when the doctor called out, "I forgot the most important thing, I'm really slipping I am."

Robert tried to picture what the woman who was privy to the phone call looked like, because she certainly had the doctor's full attention by the looks of it. He'd be forgetting his own name next.

"As I said, you don't have to be married to have children, and our Miss Nolan here is a classic example of that. The fact of the matter is she gave birth at some stage in her life."

"You are joking." Robert felt laughter bubbling up inside him.

"The fellow who planted the seed must have put two paper bags over her head." Dr Morris grinned.

"What!"

"Just in case one fell off."

"I'll invest in some, in case I need them." Robert placed his hand on the doorknob.

"Know some ugly overbearing woman, do you?" Dr Morris picked up his mobile phone and dialled a number.

CHAPTER 19

"You look extremely nice today, Ma." Greg bent down and kissed Mary Hammond on the cheek. "You smell nice too. They've used that new perfume and talcum powder I brought you." Greg beamed at the little woman who was all ready and waiting in the wheelchair for her trip to town.

After twenty minutes of pushing the wheelchair, Greg felt thirsty and decided he would have to buy a bottle of water.

It was a beautiful day for walking, and one that should be savoured because they were few and far between in Ireland, according to the old gentleman who served Greg in the newsagents. The man, now retired, had handed the business over to his son, but still helped out during the morning rush. Greg knew by the look on the man's face he wished he didn't have to work on this particular day, he really wanted to be outside like everyone else, and not trapped behind a counter.

The man turned his attention to Mary Hammond. "I know you. I can't put a name on you, but I know your face."

Greg prepared to go. He didn't want this man getting too chummy even though he appeared to be a harmless old sort.

The man suddenly remembered. "Mary Hammond, that's who you are! Are you her nephew?"

Greg gave a noncommittal smile as he exited the shop, and made a mental note not to go in there again. The last thing he needed was the third degree, because he needed to keep a low profile in the town.

Greg was really irritated, but managed to switch off and get down to the business of pushing his mother through the streets, and pointing out things he thought might interest her.

Eventually they arrived at their destination which was the cul-de-sac where Number One Eaton's Grove stood in all its majesty.

The nursing home matron had suggested it might be a good idea to take Mary to familiar places from the past, and none could be more familiar than this place, Greg thought as he eyed the blue and white police tape stretched across the front of the house.

"Do you know where you are?" Greg scrutinized his mother's face for some kind of reaction.

Her eyes were focused on the ivy twisting its way up and around the black solid front door. Despite the sun blaring down on the front of the house, it still looked cold.

"The door used to be painted brown, Ma, remember? Dark chocolate brown it was."

Mary shook her head.

Greg smiled, he was right about the colour; he could see it now in his mind's eye, so dark it was almost black.

Mary's attention was drawn back to the door.

"I've more news, Ma." Greg took *The Crier* from his pocket. "Sally Nolan has been murdered."

His eyes rested on her face. He was looking for some sort of sign that she was tuned in to what he was saying. There was no sign of comprehension, but he knew that didn't rule it out. He had read in a magazine that people in an unconscious state can hear what's being said, and the dying too, apparently; that was why sensitivity is of the utmost importance in such situations.

"Sally Nolan has been murdered," he repeated. "Her dog was killed first, that must have freaked her out somewhat. That was classy, Ma, giving her a message. That's the way the mafia do it – they let you know they are going to kill you." Greg was in full flow until he heard the tiny whimper.

"You alright, Ma?" he asked.

She looked both excited and frustrated. Then her mouth contorted, she was trying to say something.

Greg dropped to his knees in front of her.

Her thin lips parted and out came a word in two syllables "Gree... een."

Greg's mind went into overdrive, she had said a word and it sounded like 'green' but surely she wasn't talking about the door. She'd be so wrong. Then the thought occurred to him, it was the ivy, that's what she was alluding to.

"Yes, the ivy is green," Greg said. He was really happy at the show of comprehension on her part, and best of all, she'd uttered a word which could be the start of many more to come.

Mary pointed at the door.

"The door, Ma, is that what you're saying, the door was green?"

She nodded, which really disappointed him because if that was what she thought, then it was evident that she hadn't recognized the place at all.

Her pale eyes looked tired now, she was clearly spent from the activity, and he knew he was going to have to take her back to the home.

* * *

Greg spent a restless night, tossing and turning, sitting up and then lying down. He tried to stop going over and over the trip to Eaton's Grove, and that word his mother had said.

Think, think, think, his head screamed. He went over it bit by bit. He pictured himself coming home from school and going into the house. Did he go in by the front door or what?

It hit him like a ton of bricks, it was the back door that was brown; he'd always used that one, and never the front door.

He could see himself now, lifting the latch on the side gate and straight in the back door he'd go, because it was always left open.

He forced himself to visualize the front door, what colour was it? The brass knocker and letterbox, he remembered those, because once a month they'd be shined up by his Ma.

He'd arrive home from school and she'd be there with her tin of Brasso and a range of cloths, rubbing for all her worth. He would sidle up to her as she worked. Then he'd stand there amusing himself by pulling an ivy leaf and twisting it into shapes while he waited for her to finish the job.

Only when she considered that she had performed the task to the best of her ability, would she dump the Brasso and the cloths into the enamel bucket.

He always picked the bucket up and carried it for her. He'd wait at the side gate until she finished examining her handiwork.

Yes, he could see it all now. See her standing gazing at the green front door, with a big smile on her face.

Green, she was right. The front door was green, because it was his father's favourite colour.

CHAPTER 20

Robert glared across the desk at Cliff. "Do you know what we want to talk to you about?" he asked.

"I have a big function to organize for tonight, so can we get it over with? Whatever it is that's bothering you," Cliff said.

"We've had a complaint against you," Robert said.

"Someone get food poisoning, did they?" Cliff said glibly.

"Pattie Flowers said you've seriously upset her." Robert got straight to the point.

"Upset her, oh give us a bloody break, will you?"

"Would you like to call your solicitor?" Robert asked.

"Why would I want a solicitor? This is stupid."

"I don't think you realize the seriousness of the situation." Robert leant forward in his chair.

"So what situation is that then?" Cliff said.

"Sexual assault, that's what."

"You're having a laugh," Cliff retorted.

"Are you denying the complaint that's been made against you?"

"Of course I bloody well am, you moron," Cliff snapped.

95

"A doctor examined Miss Flowers, so we have the evidence."

"What kind of evidence?"

"Do you want me to spell it out to you?" Robert asked.

"Alright. Alright. She came to my place. It was late. Very late."

"And?"

"She said she'd left her scarf in the restaurant, but I knew what she really wanted, and it wasn't the scarf." Cliff sneered.

"So, tell us then, what did she want?" Robert was trying hard to keep a hold on his temper.

"To coin your own phrase, do you want me to spell it out to you?" Cliff replied.

"Yes, that's exactly what I want you to do, spell it out to me, why don't you?"

"She was gagging for it." Cliff sneered again.

Robert's blood froze, his thoughts turned to Annie. The proof that she was telling the truth about this groping bastard was staring him right in the face.

"You're a man of the world, Robert. You know when a woman wants it, or do you, I wonder? Considering you left Annie a bit short-changed in that department if you get my drift."

Robert jumped up out of the chair knocking it over in the process.

James Sayder swiftly rose to his feet and grabbed Robert by the shoulder. He turned him round and stared into his ashen face.

"He fucking disgusts me," Robert said. "He's a fucking scumbag."

"Don't, sir," James pleaded. It was obvious Robert wanted to kick the living daylights out of Cliff, even if it meant he could lose his job, and be done for assault.

Robert shot Cliff a look of contempt before turning abruptly, forcing James to release his grip.

James's shoulders relaxed as Robert made for the door. An explosive situation had been diffused and he was grateful for that.

"Can I go so?" Cliff called after Robert.

Robert swung round. "Get your solicitor here right now, because I want a fucking statement from you, and you're not leaving until I get it."

On that note Robert left the room with his heart pounding in his chest. His throat was so dry he thought he was going to choke. He filled a plastic cup with water from the dispenser in the hall and downed it in one go.

How could he possibly have been taken in by that slimy pervert Cliff? The fucker was laughing his arse off at him in there. Going on about Annie like that, and he – supposedly a friend.

It had never been the same between Annie and Robert after he'd caught Cliff with his arms around her. So, had that been Cliff's belief at the time, that Annie was gagging for it? Because what was it he was saying in there, after all? She wasn't getting enough. Robert's face burned with fury as Cliff's words rang in his ears.

Gagging for it had always been Cliff's favourite terminology. He used it as an excuse all those years ago when they were in their final year in school. There had been a young girl, who'd complained that Cliff had interfered with her, and he had boasted to the boys about his conquest using those very words. She was gagging for it.

The complaint had come to nothing though. It was all swept under the carpet.

Cliff came from a well-to-do family where money was no object. Had they paid the girl off to keep her quiet?

The truth that he had been stupidly too blind to see until now, was staring him in the face. Cliff was a danger to women and always had been, even from an early age. A sex fiend, no, it was worse than that. The fucker was a serial rapist and the really terrible thing about it was that he had been getting away with it for years.

Robert rebuked himself for having been so self-righteous and blind. Why hadn't he given Annie a hearing? Why had he dismissed her like she was a bold child telling lies? Was it possible that the Cliff fucker raped her too? The thought of it sickened him. How could he have been so stupid? Wasn't that the story of his life though, going around with his head up his arse, blaming the whole world for his apathy and his bloody miserable existence?

He remembered a book he'd read years ago, 'life is about acceptance' had been the main theme. He hadn't agreed with the theory at all, but he was inclined to agree with it now. Acceptance was the key, and the sooner he could start practicing that principle, the sooner he could start living.

CHAPTER 21

"You've had a rough few days," Maggie told Pattie. "Why don't you stay here with me, for tonight at least?"

"Yes, I think I might do that."

"You could have a nice bath, it'll relax you," Maggie suggested. "I have to go back to *The Crier*, only for a while though, but I'm sure you'll be fine here."

"Yes, a good soak will do me good," Pattie agreed.

"Use whatever you want," Maggie said as she made her way out. "I bought a new facemask, you should try it, and there's a nice bottle of red in the kitchen opened and waiting to be poured."

Pattie was soon relaxing in a bath full of bubbles. She felt so relaxed that she dozed off. For how long she didn't know, but the water was still warm and soothing when she woke.

She dried herself with a luxurious white bath towel, and encased her hair in a smaller one before fashioning it into a turban. The bathrobe Maggie had left out for her was equally luxurious. Maggie certainly had good taste, she reasoned. She applied the facemask crème to her face noting its cooling effect on her skin. She'd have to buy a tub for herself, she vowed as she made her way from the bathroom to the kitchen.

"A glass of wine won't go amiss," she stated aloud as she poured out a generous glass. She had come to like wine, Maggie had won her over. Slowly she made her way into the sitting room.

This is such a nice cosy place; Maggie is so lucky, she thought enviously as she put the glass down on the mantelpiece and viewed herself in the ornate mirror.

The face mask was starting to harden and Pattie tried not to smile at her reflection. She looked like a statue – a green one.

After taking a sip of wine she started to relax, all she had to do now was keep the memory of that awful event, with that wicked fellow, out of her head. It was so brutal the way he attacked her, but she'd have to have faith in the law and hope and pray that justice would be done.

When she had told Robert Carroll she was going to make a formal complaint, he seemed quite pleased about it, which prompted her to think that there must have been other victims who'd suffered at the hands of that animal. She couldn't even say his name she was so disgusted with him. And to think that she had thought he was the bee's knees.

She took another sip of the wine before looking back into the mirror. She froze when she saw the reflection of a hooded figure behind her own.

Swinging round she spilt the wine on herself. She felt the liquid on her skin, and the jammy smell rise to her nostrils.

"What are you doing here?" she croaked.

There was no reply from the visitor.

"You want to frighten me into dropping the charges, don't you?" She felt a queasiness creep into her throat. "I know it's you, Cliff."

Still no reply came.

She was in a complete state of panic. "Say something," she screeched.

The hooded figure was standing perfectly still, which was intimidating in itself.

"You are an evil man," Pattie said angrily and eyed the door. She could make a run for it, she realized, but how far would she get before he'd overpower her?

As if he had read her mind, the hoodie turned and walked towards the door.

Pattie came to the conclusion that he was going to lock the door and attack her again. A determination now welled up inside her. She would stop him no matter what it was she had to do. Turning back to the mantelpiece she eyed the wooden statue of an elephant, she knew it was heavy because she'd picked it up earlier. She could use it as a weapon to protect herself; she would give him a right good whack with it, because there was no way she was letting him get away with it this time.

She laid the glass down and picked up the ornament but as she swung round to face her would be attacker, she realized with dismay that she'd lost her footing. Desperately, she grappled to catch onto something for support, but failed miserably.

The hooded figure stood and watched a helpless Pattie Flowers falling. There was a loud crack as her head hit the hearth, and the blood that was spilling out of her screamed out the obvious.

* * *

Greg Joubert threw himself down on his bed as soon as he got back to his camper van.

What in God's name was that woman doing in Forge Cottage? he fumed. He had seen Maggie Lehane driving off, and thought it was perfectly safe to let himself into the cottage, like he had done on several other occasions.

He had got a real shock when he saw a figure emerging from the bathroom with a green face of all things. He had managed to hide himself down behind the settee with the intention of leaving as soon as it was safe. But no, the cute bitch had to spot him, didn't she? She saw his reflection in the mirror as he tried to creep out of the room. Anyway, now that he thought about it, what the hell was she doing gawping at herself in that state for? She looked like something from outer space.

There was nothing he could do for her, he knew, there was no point in calling an ambulance because there was nothing they could do either. She was a goner the minute her head cracked open. He reckoned she'd died instantly which was a blessing for her, and for him too, though if she had survived she couldn't have named him. He knew she didn't recognize him because she had called him by some other name, Cliff, whoever he was. By the sounds of it, that fellow was in severe trouble.

Stupid, stupid woman, he could have done without that little episode. He jumped up from the bed. He had a bottle of cooking wine somewhere in the cupboard, and he was going to drink every drop of it no matter how foul it tasted.

CHAPTER 22

"You can't stay here," Robert told Maggie. "This is a crime scene."

Maggie was standing motionless, staring down at Pattie's body.

"We need to get the boys to do their work." Robert went up a tone, when he realized she was oblivious to his words.

Laying his hands on her shoulders he gently turned her away from the pitiful scene and repeated what he'd just said.

This time she comprehended his urging. "Yes, you're right." Her voice trembled with emotion.

"I'll take you to the hotel," Robert said.

"I hate hotels." Maggie was adamant she wasn't going to spend the night in a room in the run-down Imperial.

"So, have you a friend to stay with?" Robert asked.

"You can stay at mine if you like," James Sayder interjected.

"Your pokey little flat," Robert joked. "How could she stay in that cupboard?"

"Thank you for your offer," Maggie nodded at James. She gave Robert a look which intimated she considered his light-heartedness inappropriate under the circumstances.

"There's nothing wrong with my flat," James said.

"I'm sure it'll be just fine and thanks again," Maggie said.

"It's just round the corner from *The Crier*." James ignored the look of annoyance on Robert's face.

"I didn't know there were flats on Church Street," Maggie remarked.

"Do you know the jeweller's shop? Well, my place is at the back of it and it's all newly decorated with my own entrance. The landlady, Miss Duffner, wouldn't mind you staying the night. She's very open-minded for a woman in her seventies. Not of course that I've had people staying already." James blushed.

"I've been to Duffner's to get my alarm clock repaired." Maggie was momentarily distracted from the bizarre situation of Pattie's body lying just a few yards away.

"And I've been into his flat, you couldn't swing a cat in there, no, you'd be better off at my place," Robert insisted.

Realizing Robert was determined to get his own way in the matter, James cocked his head sideways and gave him a knowing look.

Maggie had turned away and was slowly trudging out into the hall.

Robert followed her out with James lapping at his heels.

"Won't you need to take some night things?" Robert prompted.

"I won't be sleeping; your couch will do me fine," Maggie assured him.

"OK," Robert placated her.

"I just need to be away from all this madness."

On dropping Robert and Maggie off, James threw Robert another one of his knowing looks.

"What's your problem?" Robert asked through clenched teeth.

"See you in the morning, sir," James winked and drove off.

Robert fumbled in his pocked for his keys before joining Maggie on the doorstep.

"Would you like a hot drink?" Robert asked.

"No, I'm fine."

He pointed the way to the sitting room. "A proper drink maybe."

When Maggie didn't answer, he presumed it might mean a maybe.

Maggie had seated herself and Robert placed an unopened bottle of cognac and a jug of water on the coffee table in front of her.

"I'm afraid I haven't any soft drink to mix in with it, sorry it's got to be water," he said.

"Water's fine."

Robert took two crystal glasses from the box set of six. The lads at the station had presented them to himself and Annie as an engagement present. Quickly he blotted out the memory by concentrating on pouring a generous measure of the golden liquid into each glass.

They sat in silence for a few minutes, Robert drinking his cognac neat as always, and Maggie staring down at hers. Eventually she reached out for the glass, which was glistening in all its newness.

"I suppose one won't kill me," she said quietly and she raised the glass to her lips.

"Are you going to water it down?" Robert pointed to the jug. "It might be a bit too strong for you," he warned.

To his surprise she downed the drink in one go.

"I needed that." She sounded instantly relaxed.

Robert offered a refill and she didn't refuse.

"Pattie was murdered, wasn't she?" Maggie said.

"We'll know more in the next few days," Robert replied.

"It's a serial killer," Maggie said.

"A serial killer here, in this little town." Robert laughed softly. "That's a ridiculous idea if you don't mind me saying so."

"Yes, that's what this is all about, isn't it? We have a serial killer operating here in Magnerstown," Maggie said as she inwardly wrestled with her conscience. Should she tell him about the photos of Sally Nolan and her dog? It was obvious the killer took them.

"We don't want to go jumping to conclusions," Robert said as he refilled his glass.

"I was the intended victim, wasn't I?" Maggie was not letting up. The idea had now entered her head that the photos could have been a warning that she was going to be the next victim. But what had she done wrong? Whom had she upset? If only she could tell this man beside her what she knew, but she couldn't, because deep down in her heart she couldn't trust him with that kind of information. In any case, if she did tell him, she'd probably be charged with withholding information. It was bad when you couldn't put your faith in a policeman.

"Look, you shouldn't be distressing yourself," Robert said.

"Or else it could be that it was Pattie who was the target and not me." Maggie took a gulp from the glass she had been cradling against her chest.

"There's no point in speculating at this point," Robert said.

"It was Cliff." Maggie gasped as the idea hit her.

"Why would he want to kill Pattie?" Robert asked.

"To stop her pursuing the complaint she had against him." Maggie was convinced that was the explanation.

"Wouldn't killing her be a bit of an extreme measure to stop her?"

Maggie finished the contents of her glass before giving him an answer. "Maybe you're right." But the edge in her voice implied she wasn't fully accepting Robert's reasoning.

They sat side by side in silence until Robert felt Maggie's head seek out his shoulder.

He stared straight ahead with his mind working overtime.

After much internal debate, he turned his head sideways to look at her, and to his utter surprise he discovered she was fast asleep.

He laughed at himself for surmising that she had deliberately put her head there. What was he thinking? That she fancied him? It was the complete opposite in fact. She hated him. She had made that quite plain.

Gently he pulled away from her. She opened her eyes for a brief second, and then she lay down, tucking her legs under her in order to fit in the small space.

He stood listening to her slow, easy breathing for a minute. Then, quietly, he crept away to his bedroom taking the remains of the bottle of cognac and his glass with him.

CHAPTER 23

"So where were you on Monday night, Cliff?"

Cliff shook his head in disbelief. "I can't believe you think I had anything to do with this murder business," he said.

"You had a motive," Robert said.

"You have to be joking," Cliff replied.

"There is the case of sexual assault against you, or had you forgotten?" Robert snapped. "Lucky for you that's past tense now."

"Come on, Robbie, the woman grossly exaggerated that situation out of all proportion."

"They seem to have a habit of doing that, don't they?"

"I'm not following you," Cliff said.

"I'm just thinking back to our schooldays, remember those?"

"What are you going to come out with now?" Cliff grinned. "Cheat at the exams, did I?"

"Remember that young girl, what was her name?"

"What are you talking about now?"

"Betty Tobin, that was her name, nice shy little thing she was too, if my memory serves me right."

"Don't remember." Cliff feigned confusion.

"Your first victim." Robert tapped the desk with his pen. "Did she exaggerate too, in your opinion that is?"

"Surely you didn't believe that cock-and-bull story." Cliff laughed.

"I didn't know what to think at the time, but now I know exactly what went on," Robert replied.

"And you are supposed to be my best friend."

Robert looked straight into Cliff's eyes and picked up on the anxiety gathering there.

"We are still friends, aren't we?" Cliff said.

"That Tobin made it all up, just to get money," Cliff waved his hand dismissively. "A right rough lot her family. They saw the opportunity to make a few pounds and they took it."

"It was rumoured she got money. They said your old man paid her off to save your slimy skin," Robert said.

"I could have you for slander, friend or no friend," Cliff sneered.

"You always had a big gob, Cliff. You mouthed off to the boys how she was gagging for it. If a case had been taken against you, you'd have buried yourself."

Cliff pounded the desk with his fist. "You sanctimonious bastard," he said.

"So, was that what you were up to on Monday night then, buying your way out of another hole you'd dug yourself into?"

"You think I murdered the Flowers woman; I can't believe you're that bloody stupid."

"Yes, you're so right about the stupid bit, only that's all in the past now. I was stupid then, know what I mean?"

Cliff laughed uneasily.

"Do I have to ask you again, about Monday night?"

"I was at home."

"Who with?"

"Nobody."

"So, you have no witness to verify that."

"Look Robbie, I was tired, I went to bed early, you know how it is. The business is hard going, unlike your job, whatever that is."

Robert fumbled in the desk drawer for paper trying hard to ignore Cliff's jibe. "I'll have to take a statement from you," he said.

Cliff's jovial mood suddenly changed. "I want my solicitor here," he said.

"Sure," Robert agreed. Then turning to James Sayder, he instructed him to ring Mr Carter Jones.

James shot Robert a warning look as he made to leave the room. He knew Robert had made it clear during the last interview that he despised Cliff for some reason or other, and here they were again in exactly the same situation. There was the possibility that Robert might lose his head as soon as he found himself alone with the man. He could do something that might land him in a lot of trouble. The angry confrontation had been diffused the last time, but only just.

Picking up on James's apprehension, Robert assured him nothing would happen. "It'll be alright, he's not worth it, I know," he said.

As soon as the door closed behind James, Robert turned his attention back to Cliff. He stared long and hard at him before speaking. "Annie, remember her?"

"Aw come on, Robbie, this is what this little charade is all about, isn't it?"

"She was right, you are a danger to women," Robert said. "I know that now."

Cliff seemed uncomfortable for a minute, but quickly gathered himself. "Let's not drag all that sorry business up again. Anyway, I did you a favour, because you and Annie were going nowhere."

"Now this is for your ears only, Cliffy boy," Robert said through clenched teeth. "I'll see to it that you are kept in gaol until your trial. I'll pull every trick in the book to stop you getting bail. I'll make sure you share a cell with the worst kind of scumbag in the place, you'll be afraid to piss crooked."

"I don't think so." Cliff dismissed Robert's threat with a wave of his hand. "Money talks, you know. Money fucking roars."

Robert sank back down into his chair and opened his hands under the desk. He could see the print of his nails on his upturned palms.

"Shouldn't you have a tape on or something?" Cliff laughed sarcastically.

"This is a small town, we do things differently here." Robert retorted.

"I'll be getting my solicitor to look into that," Cliff said triumphantly. "You can't get away with threatening me, even if it is in private."

Robert seethed with anger but just about managed to contain himself, he was an inch away from getting up and punching Cliff in his smarmy face.

"Where is the superintendent? He wouldn't be pleased if he knew you had me in here treating me like a common criminal."

"He's one of your little golfing buddies no doubt, the *crème de la crème* hobnobbing in all the right places."

"You got that right, Mr Detective, or whatever you are. The super and I are acquainted as it happens," Cliff admitted.

"Too bad he's not here to hold your hand then, pity he's away on a little break as it happens." Robert mimicked Cliff's tone.

"Easy known he's not around, because he wouldn't allow this kind of harassment to take place."

"I know," Robert replied.

"You piss artist, you've engineered all this." Cliff went white with anger. "You're only doing this to get back at me over that daft Annie bitch."

Robert stood up knocking the chair over, he didn't care about the consequences, and he was going to do what he should have done ages ago, beat the shit out of this high-class scumbag.

James Sayder rushed back into the room before Robert could make a move on Cliff and grabbed him by the shoulder.

Robert sensed from the look on James's face that there had been some new developments. "What is it?" he asked.

"The post-mortem results are in," James obliged.

"And?"

"It was an accident."

Robert retrieved the chair and sat down heavily with disbelief written all over his face.

"You are free to go," James told Cliff because he knew Robert was too dumbfounded to bring himself to speak.

CHAPTER 24

Cliff threw open his wardrobe door and perused its contents before selecting a few items and placing them on the bed. He was still angry with Robert Carroll; how dare he make a show of him like that in that crummy little run-down cop shop? Then, all those people standing outside the bloody place, looking at him like he was a common criminal or something.

How did that lot of onlookers happen to be in the vicinity? he wondered. It was as if word had gone out there'd been an arrest in connection with the Flowers woman's death.

It was a wonder that Mickey Mouse of a paper crowd weren't there too with their cheap little camera.

Cliff strode out onto the landing and opened a door where he stored his suitcases. He pushed the golf clubs aside and grabbed a small leather bag which would do the job because he wouldn't be taking much with him. The garb he needed for where he was going would already be in situ.

While packing, he made a mental note of what he had to do next. Book a flight and then send an email to his housekeeper in Spain instructing her to get the villa ready for his impending arrival, but the most important thing which would have to be done first and foremost, was to ring the restaurant and tell the very-capable Pieter he was being promoted to taking charge of the place until further notice.

At least he could depend on some people for loyalty. Unlike the man who was supposed to be his friend, and the way he was prepared to betray him.

It was all jealousy on Carroll's part. He was nothing but a loser. He hadn't even got a woman. What was he after all? Only an old has-been in a dead-end job with no prospects.

Hurriedly Cliff made his way to his study. "He's a loser, and he's not going to drag me down with him," he said aloud.

CHAPTER 25

"Pattie was not murdered," Maggie echoed Robert's words.

"That's good news, isn't it?" Robert said. Instinctively he felt uncomfortable with the way it came out. How could it be good news? Pattie Flowers was dead after all.

"So, Cliff gets off with the assault."

"Her death was just an accident." Robert cringed at his choice of the word – just.

"I shouldn't have left her alone," Maggie said. "It's my fault she's dead, I'm to blame for this whole sorry mess."

"Don't be silly," Robert replied. "Even if you had been there, she could still have fallen, and there would have been nothing you could have done for her. Dr Morris said death was instantaneous."

"Couldn't someone have broken into the house and frightened her?" Maggie asked.

"There was no sign of a break in. Weren't you the first on the scene? You said you saw nothing out of the ordinary," Robert replied.

"So that's the conclusion then, an accident?"

"An accident," Robert agreed.

"This might sound strange, but I'm actually disappointed that it wasn't murder," Maggie admitted.

"Yes, indeed murder would make for better headlines alright."

Maggie looked at Robert with undisguised contempt. "I wasn't thinking along those lines," she said.

Robert shifted uneasily wondering why he'd been so foolish in making such a suggestion in the first place. "I shouldn't have said that," he admitted.

"You're quite right, you shouldn't have said it," Maggie replied.

"I need to talk to your journalist chap about Sally Nolan," said Robert, changing the subject.

"Joey Tyrell. What on Earth for?"

"He was spotted hanging around her house by someone out walking, and we think your man might have been the last person to see her alive."

"So, is he a suspect then?" Maggie asked. She wanted this Robert fellow out of her sight, because he was getting right up her nose, and she was developing a very strong desire to slap his face, but she resisted. He would probably arrest her for assault, the wimp.

"Everyone's a suspect," Robert said flippantly. But, seeing the reaction on Maggie's face, he realized he was digging himself even further down into the big hole he'd already created.

Maggie scribbled on a Post-It Note and threw it across the desk at him with a vengeance.

"That's Joey's address," she said. She proceeded to rustle through some papers, then wrote something down on a notepad. "That it then?" She intimated that she wanted him to take himself out of her sight immediately if not sooner.

"I'll see myself out so, will I?" Robert asked.

There was no reply, just an icy stare.

Trying to hide his embarrassment, Robert stood up. He'd stepped on her toes with his big hobnail boots this time, just when he thought he was getting on her good side.

He was good at mucking things up with women, he admitted to himself as he made his way out onto the street.

He thought about Annie, and how he'd taken Cliff's side and not hers when she tried to explain things. He'd been so unfair to the woman. He would have to write to her and apologize. But then realization dawned on him, he hadn't an address for her, nor a phone number come to think of it. So that was another thing he was good at, the business of severing all ties.

CHAPTER 26

"Thank you for coming in, Mr Tyrell, please sit down," Robert said.

"I hope you didn't get one of the squad car fellows to deliver your note," Joey snapped.

"Have you a problem with that?" Robert bent forward.

"Yes, I have a huge problem with it. I don't want the neighbours jumping to wrong conclusions," Joey replied.

"I got your address from your editor," Robert said.

"You went to see Maggie Lehane, did you?" Joey asked. What had she disclosed to this dick? he wondered; he would have to play it cool, give as little as possible away. He was well aware of how the cops worked in order to trip people up by pretending they'd got information out of a co-conspirator or witness. Then if you were brainless enough, you'd blab it all out. Sing like a canary, in other words.

"Yeah, I went to see your boss," Robert replied.

"So, what is this all about then?" Joey asked.

"Sally Nolan."

"What about her?"

"You went to see her."

"Did I?" Joey played dumb.

"You were seen outside her place taking a photograph, and I have a witness to that effect."

That confirmed it for Joey, Maggie hadn't told the dick about the story he'd been sent to get. It looked like she'd given no information at all, the clever woman, and for that he admired her.

"Well?" Robert prompted.

"I did take a photo of the Nolan woman's house, to be honest. I paint, you see, so I thought I might do a picture of the place and sell it to her. I do that, you see. Would you like one done?"

"So, you were just out to make a fast buck, is that it?"

"That's it in a nutshell." Joey grinned.

"Did you talk to Miss Nolan about your plan for the painting you intended to do?"

"No, I didn't talk to her about the painting," Joey replied. Twisted as it might sound, he was telling the truth. He hadn't talked to her about such a venture at all, and he knew by the look on Robert's face that he had no option but to believe him.

CHAPTER 27

When Robert Carroll and James Sayder arrived at the cemetery, the funeral of Pattie Flowers was well underway.

Robert pulled James back. "Let's stay here," he said. "We don't want to appear disrespectful arriving so late."

Toby Jackson raised his hand in salutation to the two detectives and proceeded to lock the big silver gates behind them. The mourners would be leaving by the turnstile, which was fine considering there were so few of them anyway, and the hearse had already departed, its work done.

In the distance Robert spotted the unmistakable figure of Maggie Lehane amongst the small group huddled around the grave.

"You'd think there would have been a bigger turnout, seeing as Pattie Flowers was so well-known in the town," Robert remarked.

"That's because she wasn't a vegetarian, there would have been a big turnip at her funeral if she was."

"Got that one in a Christmas cracker did you, James?" Robert frowned.

"I believe Cliff's taken himself off to Spain," James said. "That Polish waiter, I can't remember his name–"

"Pieter," Robert prompted.

"Yes Pieter; he is real proud of running the place, and he has told the whole town about his promotion."

"Doesn't surprise me that Cliff would do something sneaky like abandoning ship, he was always ahead of the posse, that fellow," Robert said.

The sound of keys dropping on concrete attracted their attention to Toby. He looked at them apologetically and mouthed 'sorry.'

"He can't wait to get away for a pint," James whispered.

Robert rubbed his hands together; it was a damp misty day, typical funeral weather. "Can't say I blame him, it is a Sunday after all," he said.

James walked back to Toby.

"You're an important man with all those keys," James began.

"I'm like a gaoler," Toby joked. "Mind you I could be minus one key soon," he added.

"How's that then?" James asked.

"There's a rumour going around that the courthouse is going to close down," Toby replied.

"Why's that?" James asked.

"Ah you know yourself, the place is so old and dilapidated. Isn't it just like something from Charles Dickens?"

"That's true," James agreed. "You'd nearly expect to see Tiny Tim limping round the corner."

"I mean to say it must be the only building in the country with toilets out in the backyard," Toby said. "I'm an easy-going type of fellow, but that takes the biscuit in this day and age."

"You're quite right," James said. "The building should be condemned because it's just not up to snuff."

"Now that Judge Mangan is out of the picture it would make sense to send the few cases they have over to Vitalstown."

"Few cases is right; the judge wasn't exactly run off his feet," James agreed.

"Old Mangan was good for a tip though, not like that tight arse they're sending over from Vitalstown to fill in for the moment," Toby said.

"I should imagine you're going to miss those little perks now," James replied.

"I won't miss cutting Mangan's grass though; miles of it he has, or should I say had… You know it used to take me the whole of a Saturday to get it done. I'd start at seven in the morning and finish at six. Twice a month I used to have to do it. The other two Saturdays would be taken up with the garden. The weeding was backbreaking, and cutting hedges and all the other stuff was a full day's work as well."

"Judge Mangan was an early riser then, seeing you started at seven every Saturday morning."

"God no, I had a key to the place."

"Really!"

"He gave me a free hand the judge did, except for one little disagreement we had."

"And what was that?" James asked.

"I like to put a bet on the horses you see, and Saturday's a great day for it, so I asked him once if I could change to a Sunday instead, but he wouldn't hear of it. He went on about Sunday being a day of rest, real into his religion he was – which was laughable in a way, seeing he was into… ah you know what I mean… them ladies of the night and all that kind–"

James cut in on Toby's speech. "I've been to the judge's home, and you're quite right, Toby, he could have had his own private golf course with all the lawns that are out there," he said.

"Green Park was the right choice of name for the place alright," Toby replied. "A sea of green, and me swimming in the middle of it all."

"You were quite a busy man," James said before returning to Robert's side. He could see that the funeral had reached the point where the coffin was being lowered into the grave, so he remained silent for a moment out of respect before addressing Robert. "Sir," he said softly.

"Yes, I heard," Robert said.

"I've had a thought."

"Yes."

"The judge's key ring."

"What about it?"

"There were three keys on it."

"So?"

"Front door key, gate key, and car key."

"Your point being?" Robert asked.

"There was one missing," James replied.

"What are you talking about?" But James had gone back to Toby.

"Did Judge Mangan have a key to the courthouse?" James asked.

"No."

"Who else besides you has a key to the building?" James asked.

"No one," Toby replied.

"That's a big responsibility for you."

"It is." Toby bubbled with pride.

"What would happen if you were to lose that key?" James asked.

"Replace the lock."

"That simple?"

"No, to be honest I was only joking, that would never happen because I have a few spare keys to the courthouse."

"And would I be right in thinking that you more than likely have duplicate keys to Green Park too?" James asked.

"I have indeed." Toby smiled broadly. "The key man, that's me."

The small black procession of mourners started to make their way up the path.

"It's over." Robert mouthed the warning over his shoulder.

James returned to Robert's side just a second before Maggie drew level with them both.

"How are you, Miss Lehane?" James asked reverently. Robert seemed stuck for words so it was up to him to say something.

Maggie acknowledged James with a smile of appreciation for his interest. "I'm still stunned," she admitted. "But I'll have to get on with it, won't I?"

James poked Robert in the back. "Why don't you take the lady for a drink, sir? She looks done in."

"You'd hardly want to." Robert braced himself for a refusal.

To his utter amazement she said, "Yes I will, because I want to get drunk and blot everything out."

CHAPTER 28

After dropping Robert and Maggie off at the pub, James sat for a few minutes in the car mulling things over in his mind. The first idea he came up with was how he would love to bang both Robert Carroll and Maggie Lehane's heads together in order to wake them up.

It was as plain as the nose on your face that they were a couple waiting to happen.

His thoughts reverted back to himself. He was feeling so lonely lately, mainly because everyone he knew was pairing off, leaving him the odd man out. Most of his friends were either engaged, married, or in relationships.

Even his mother had a love interest, but she didn't know he knew about it. It was owing to a number of clues that he'd figured out which led him to this discovery.

Last time he went home he noticed she had a new hairstyle, and she'd put some kind of colour into it. She had bought a few new clothes too, which were brighter and much more revealing than her usual style.

She'd left a carrier bag on the kitchen counter, probably thinking he wouldn't have a peek inside. But he did have a look, which was a first for him. It was frilly underwear stuff. He noted the lettering on the carrier bag

– Anne Summers. Wasn't that the place that sold all that sexy underwear and erotic stuff? She was entitled to do what she wanted, he reasoned after much deliberation. She was an adult and she didn't need permission.

And then there was the texting. She was worse than a teenager. One Saturday night it was text after text, and he felt like getting up and going to his room. He stuck it out though, pretending not to notice and focusing on the show on the television. She looked so happy, he didn't want to be a killjoy and spoil her fun.

Then there was the case of the new recipes she was trying out. 'If you were a man, James, what would you think of that?' she had asked after a meal she'd cooked on his last visit home.

I am a man, he'd told her. She hadn't meant it literally, she'd said.

He knew she was just testing the waters. This new man would obviously be invited for a meal, and she wanted to impress him.

There was definitely something going on. Maybe the detective business was in his blood.

James started up the car and headed back to the station. After he'd parked the car outside the building he would head back to his flat. He'd relish the walk, because he needed a bit of fresh air to clear his head.

He turned on the radio. "And that was 'Everyone's Gone to the Moon' for Martin and Sheila in Tipperary," the presenter was saying.

James laughed. That was so apt. Everyone had gone to the moon, except for him that was. His rocket had simply failed to launch.

CHAPTER 29

After her third glass of red wine in Dunworth's Pub, Maggie became lightheaded and started to regret her plan to get smashed.

"Would you mind if I went home?" she asked.

Robert dutifully dialled a taxi number on his mobile. "As a matter of fact, I'll call it a day myself and I'll share the taxi with you, if you don't mind," he said.

On arrival at Forge Cottage, Robert instructed the taxi driver to wait while he saw Maggie to the front door.

"Oh, I can't believe I've left my handbag in the pub," Maggie moaned.

"I'll go back and get it," Robert offered. "But you'll have to come too. I can't leave you here on your own."

"Why, will the bogeyman get me?" Maggie laughed as she bent down to retrieve the key from under the mat.

Robert was dumbfounded.

"Everyone in Magnerstown keeps their keys under mats and plant pots, and anything else they can put them under," Maggie said.

"But that's an open invitation to all sorts of queer folk," Robert said.

Maggie laughed at his seriousness.

Robert turned to make his way back to the taxi, but Maggie surprised him by clutching at his arm.

"Would you mind coming in for a while?" she pleaded.

Robert readily agreed and sent the taxi driver away after paying him.

Once inside the house Maggie tottered a bit unsteadily to her bedroom and threw herself still fully clothed onto the bed.

Robert stood framed in the doorway looking at her; she looked so small and fragile in the middle of that huge bed.

"I'll ring the barman and ask him to put your bag inside the counter for safekeeping," Robert said.

Maggie moaned softly.

"Anything you need in it, other than the door key, that is?" Robert laughed.

There was no reaction this time.

"You'll collect it tomorrow so," he said and then moved closer for confirmation that Maggie was sleeping peacefully.

Robert phoned the pub as promised, then let himself out and closed the front door behind him as quietly as possible. Not that it mattered how he closed it, because it would take a lot to wake Maggie up. She was exhausted, while he on the other hand was the complete opposite. He decided against phoning for the taxi to come back for him, he was in the mood for a good long walk.

Noticing Maggie's key still in the door he shook his head disapprovingly as he removed it. He bent down and returned it to its so-called hiding place and muttered under his breath. It hadn't taken her long to throw off her city robe and get into small town bad habits. As he closed the gate behind him, he was so wrapped up in his thoughts that he was totally unaware of the hooded figure watching him from the shadows.

Robert's mind went back to the day's events as he walked briskly towards home. He'd always found walking helped him to think – he'd have to do it more often, he thought.

He went over the conversation between Toby Jackson and James Sayder regarding the key to the courthouse, and it suddenly dawned on him how it could have been possible for someone to gain entry to the courthouse, but he'd have to check it out in order to confirm his suspicions.

There was no doubt about it, but James was a clever lad, he mused, as he turned into the street where Toby lived.

He happened to know Toby's house for the simple reason he'd offered to bring Toby home from the pub one night when the man had been too drunk to stand. The barman had told him where Toby lived, and he'd arranged for the squad car to help him get the poor misfortunate home safely.

Arriving at Toby's house, Robert viewed the run-down state of it and wondered why the residents' association didn't complain about it.

Toby wouldn't be in yet, he knew because he'd only be on his second or third pint by now, but then he didn't need the man, not for the job he was here to do.

There was no mat, but there was an old white enamel bucket that had seen better days. The withered remains of what had once been a geranium was sitting in hardened compost.

"Gotcha," Robert said in triumph at the sight of the key shining up at him in the moonlight when he tilted the bucket.

This was obviously how the judge's killer got into the house while Toby slept, out of it. The object of the exercise was to remove the bunch of keys containing the one the killer wanted so badly, the key to the courthouse.

After the deadly deed was done, all the killer had to do was return the keys to the unsuspecting Toby.

Yes, that's how it happened, Robert was convinced now, and he'd relate his findings to James tomorrow morning, not forgetting to praise the young man for setting the ball rolling.

His thoughts returned to Maggie who, unknown to him, was sleeping soundly much to the delight of the hooded figure who had let himself into the cottage.

The hoodie lay down beside her on the bed, and watched her chest rise and fall. She was beautiful, he agonized, and her perfume reminded him of heady summer nights in the Mother City.

He had a hunger for her, but he wasn't going to touch her, he never would, because he didn't need to go that far.

He sighed with pleasure. Lying here beside her was gratification enough for him.

CHAPTER 30

Robert related his findings of the previous night to James Sayder, who was kind enough not to say that he had already come to that conclusion.

"So, our killer lured Judge Mangan to the courthouse having gained access with Toby's keys," James said.

"Then there's the Sally Nolan situation; what was the connection there, James?"

"Oh yes, sir, I made a bit of a discovery about Miss Nolan," James answered. He had found out how Sally Nolan and the judge knew one another and was mindful how to deliver the information because he didn't want Robert to feel upstaged.

Robert was very interested. "Go on, the suspense is killing me."

"Sally Nolan used to work for Judge Mangan, years ago."

"Really?"

"As we already know, she worked in a solicitor's office here in town for a few years before retiring."

"Old Carter Jones, that was whom she worked for, but she left when his son took over. Young Jones was probably a bit too modern for her. You could see where she was coming from," Robert reasoned.

"I actually called Carter Jones's office with the intention of talking to the boss. But I didn't have to, there was a nice receptionist there, and she was very helpful."

"Was she now!" Robert said. "Could this be love?"

James, ignoring Robert's jibe, went on with the explanation. "Apparently, our judge had his own legal business which he ran from home. That was before he was elevated to his higher position."

Robert mulled over the information.

"And guess where Mangan's home was, sir."

"Green Park."

"Before he moved there I meant. You'll never guess."

"Indulge me."

"None other than Number One Eaton's Grove, sir," James said triumphantly.

"Some connection, wouldn't you say, and you don't have to keep calling me, sir, you know?"

"So, the thing is, what did the judge and Miss Nolan do to our killer to make him want them both to die a horrible death?"

"You're presuming the killer is a man," Robert said.

"Sorry, sir," James replied.

"Did Sally Nolan buy the house from the judge, then?" Robert wondered.

James's mobile pipped, someone had sent him a text.

"I'm working on that, sir," he said as he read the message.

"Or else it could be that she didn't buy it, but she was to inherit the place after his death," Robert surmised. "So, who gets the house now?"

"I'm working on that too, sir," James replied as he typed out the message to Carter Jones's receptionist saying he was available for a drink.

"Great stuff, James, I think we deserve a nice lunch now after all that work." Robert grinned. "And listen,

James, how many more times am I going to have to ask you to lose the sir?"

CHAPTER 31

Katie Manning searched her wardrobe for something to wear for the Friday night out. She had reluctantly promised to go for a drink with Mark, her workmate. She hated the prospect of spending the night in a pub, firstly because she didn't drink and there was only so much Coke a person could stomach, and secondly there was never any talent there. Why did she have to be living and working in the most boring town in the country? Boring aside from the recent murders, that was. She would much prefer to go for a meal, but Mark didn't do meals. They were a right pair, she didn't do drink and he did, she would love to do men but there were none about, and that was the only thing that Mark and herself agreed on, there were no decent men in town, not even for him.

The green top and the black skirt, now how about that? she wondered as she held them up against her. The black skirt looked like something you'd see on a waitress, and the green top would be grand if it was St. Patrick's Day.

She would have to have a right overhaul of her clobber.

The black trousers and the black silk top, how about that? she mused. All dressed in black, he won't be coming back – Chris Rea's song came to mind.

Fool, if you think it's over, that's a laugh, Katie thought as she hummed the tune. It hadn't even begun, so how could it be over? she stopped abruptly.

What about the white blouse and the black skirt, or even the black trousers? She did a penguin impression, and that said it all, she concluded.

Katie threw herself down on the bed. Why was she getting so het up? It wasn't as if there would be anyone there. She could walk in wearing a sack and nobody would notice. She could even walk in there naked and nobody would notice, except maybe for some do-gooder who would offer her his jacket.

She could ring Mark and tell him she had a headache. That wouldn't be fair though, he was looking forward to tonight. He needed to chill out, he'd said, and after a few slippery nipples he wouldn't care if the roof caved in.

How in the name of all that's holy could he drink those cocktail yokes? They looked like a barium meal. She'd told him that, and he'd said the Coke she drank looked like muddy water.

She jumped up and went back to the wardrobe. She grabbed her spotty blouse and black trousers and threw them on the bed. No more negotiation, the ensemble had been picked and that was an end to it.

A bit of slap on the face and she was ready to go.

CHAPTER 32

James sat down on a black leather sofa next to a low table. A candle burning in a red glass container on the table was sending out a warm glow. The lights were low, and soft classical music was playing discretely in the background. He was nicely chilled out when his companion joined him.

"Hi, James." She smiled down at him.

"Patricia." James smiled back. "What would you like to drink?"

"Half a lager would do nicely." Patricia sat down after moving a cushion out of the way. She hated cushions; in her opinion, they did the exact opposite to what they were supposed to do.

James returned with the requested drink and an orange juice for himself.

"So, tell me, dearest James, what are you doing work experience with the cops for if you're studying law?" Patricia asked.

"My uncle unfortunately doesn't own a solicitor's firm, he's just a mere cop; well, he's not just mere, he's the superintendent," James said.

"Still it can't do any harm to experience the law from the grassroots," Patricia remarked.

James had clapped his eyes on the pretty blonde sitting on a high stool at the bar. She appeared to be in deep conversation with her male companion.

Patricia, noticing his interest, shouted, "Hi, Katie; hi, Mark."

Katie turned and waved back. She gave James the once over, then looked away.

She had the most incredible green-blue eyes, James noticed, and far away as they were, they shone like beacons in the night.

"So, what is it you want me to tell you?" Patricia got right down to business.

"Do you know that girl?" James's concentration was broken now.

"Her name's Katie Manning, and she is a nurse." Patricia patted James on the back. "Want me to introduce you?" she whispered.

"No," James answered. "I was only wondering, that's all."

"She's unattached," Patricia said.

"Really?" James brightened at the revelation.

"The fellow that's with her actually works with her, and he is as gay as a three-pound note, for your information."

James changed the subject because he didn't want Patricia to pick up on his interest in Katie, just in case she called her over and embarrassed the hell out of him. "What I was wondering was, do you know much about Sally Nolan, and the house she lived in? Did she own or rent it? That sort of thing," he said.

"No, she didn't own it, there was a contract saying she could live in the house for the rest of her life free of charge. I expect Judge Mangan was just paying her back for her loyalty," Patricia replied.

"Very generous of him, I must say."

"I did a very bold thing," Patricia said.

"Oh yes, what was that then?"

"I had a look at his will."

"Brilliant," James enthused.

"Everything goes to a Sister Mary Aloysius."

"The nun gets it all?"

"She's his sister."

"His sister?" James echoed in complete surprise. "The sister is his sister – that's neat."

"Do you want her address?" Patricia asked.

"Actually, we know her address."

"You do?"

"She lives in a convent in Cape Town, we found letters from her in the judge's home, but there was no indication that they were related."

"You will not, of course, disclose who you got your information from," Patricia said solemnly. "I'd be sacked on the spot."

"I'll be telling my boss, but he won't mention you supplied the information, it'll all be strictly confidential," James replied.

"I looked at Sally Nolan's will too," Patricia said.

"You are incorrigible, you are," James laughed.

"Guess who's going to benefit."

"The dog's home," James replied.

"Not at all, the church gets all her dosh, and they need it so badly don't they?" Patricia scoffed.

"So she had no relations by the looks of it, apart from Bonnie, now sadly deceased."

"Bonnie?"

"Her dog."

"I hate dogs, they bring me out in goosebumps," Patricia said.

James laughed. "It's cats that freak me out."

Patricia rose to her feet. "Well, I've got places to go to, people to see, things to do and all that jazz."

"Thanks for everything, you've been very helpful," James said.

"And you, my dearest, James, have got some talking to do." Patricia smiled as she stepped out of the way of the approaching Katie.

"His name is James," was Patricia's parting shot.

"If Mohammed does not go to the mountain," Katie grinned as she seated herself beside James, "then the mountain has to go to Mohammed."

James smiled broadly. "Hello, Mountain."

"Hello, Mohammed," Katie replied.

"It was actually supposed to be said the other way around, you know," James said matter-of-factly.

"I'm Katie, and life's too short for Bible lessons." She smiled as she placed her half-finished glass of Coke on the table.

"I know your name is Katie, and you're quite right, life is too short for any kind of lessons."

Katie eyed his untouched orange drink. "So, what are you up to now?" she asked.

"I'm going to drink this and then go home," James replied.

"That's exactly what I'm doing too," Katie said. "I'm on duty early in the morning."

"Can I... would you..." James struggled with what he wanted to say.

"Would I like you to see me home, is that it?" Katie asked.

"You've read my mind," James said meekly.

"I thought you'd never ask, James." Katie's green-blue eyes were twinkling with merriment.

CHAPTER 33

Judge Mangan's funeral went ahead at last, and it turned out to be a huge affair. It looked like every legal eagle in the country had converged on Magnerstown to see the man off to his eternal reward.

The judge's sister was conspicuous by her absence, but her excuse for non-attendance was well in the mix. It was a long journey from South Africa to Ireland, and it was decided by the abbess of the convent that Sister Aloysius was far too frail to travel, but seemingly not – according to some of the attendees who weren't afraid to call a spade a spade – too frail to arrange for her brother's properties to be put up for sale.

The estate agents were advertising the impending auctions of the two houses before the judge had even taken up residence in his grave.

There wasn't much money to play with though, apparently gambling and the ladies claimed most of that, or such was the rumour going around.

"Wasn't it lucky for the delicate Sister Mary Aloysius that her brother didn't live to the stage of re-mortgaging his properties in order to feed his habits?" Robert made the observation as he and James made their way to the funeral function which was to be held in Cliff's Restaurant.

The restaurant was packed to capacity with sympathizers and Robert and James had to weave their way through the crowd.

A long table adorned with glasses of wine and bottles of mineral water took centre place.

James helped himself to a bottle of water and a glass of red wine for Robert, but he was met with a glare rather than a thank you for his pains.

"Is that all they've got? Bloody altar wine." Robert mouthed his displeasure.

"The blood of Christ." James laughed. "You're right though, it's a bit of a cheap do alright. I suppose she didn't want to—"

"Who?" Robert butted in.

"The sister in South Africa's obviously paying for this," James said.

"Won't she be getting a small fortune for the Green Park mansion?" Robert retorted.

"And the Eaton's Grove house; posh place like that will fetch a nice tidy sum," James added.

"We'll mingle and listen," Robert said.

"I bet half of this lot didn't even know him," James ventured.

"Funeral groupies," Robert replied. "Jesus Christ, is this vinegar in disguise?" He scowled after taking a sip of the wine.

James pointed over to the far corner, "There's Dr Morris,"

"Who's the man with him?" Robert wondered as he surveyed the small grey-haired companion.

"Isn't he the fellow who gave the eulogy?" James answered.

"Honour among thieves," Robert said knowingly as he glanced around taking in the guests.

"Will they serve any food, do you think?"

"You hungry, James?"

"Ish."

"Why don't you go and find out when the grub's up?" Robert urged.

James did as he was told, only to return with an expression which told Robert there would be no chance of any sustenance coming their way.

Robert turned his attention back to the corner and discovered that Dr Morris had departed and someone else had taken his place. The grey-haired man had changed seats, and all that could be seen of him now was the back of his head.

"Who's that with our man now?" Robert asked.

James screwed up his eyes in an effort to try and figure out who the grey-haired man's companion was. "Can't see his face with the hood he's got on," James replied.

"Bloody hoodies – should be a law against it."

"There is, sir, but not here in Magnerstown, though." James laughed. "There's a small bit of catching up to do here, wouldn't you agree, sir?"

Robert threw James a look before taking another gulp of the wine. "This is painful."

"I agree, it's cheap and nasty," Dr Morris's voice boomed out from behind them.

"I thought you'd gone," Robert stated.

"Had to make a phone call."

Robert looked back to the corner and noted that the hoodie had departed.

Dr Morris pointed to the grey head in the corner. "I've just been talking to the psychiatrist I was telling you about, Dr Curtin. You did say you wanted to meet him, didn't you?"

"Yes, I'd like to hear what he has to say about this patricide theory of his." Robert followed the doctor with James in hot pursuit.

Dr Morris stopped dead in his tracks. "Oh my giddy aunt," he said.

Robert stared in disbelief at the red gash and the blood spill.

Dr Curtin was sporting the same neck that the judge and Sally Nolan had done.

"Right under our noses. Can you just credit it?" James said.

"Thank God there's nobody over here to see this," Dr Morris said.

Robert felt a hand on his shoulder and turned round to find a smiling Joey Tyrell armed with a camera. "Mind if I get in there?" he asked. Not waiting for an answer, he pushed through and started loading up his camera.

"The nerve of him," Robert uttered.

Joey continued undaunted.

"You can't take photos. This is a crime scene," Robert protested.

"Better get the old crime scene tape out then, hadn't you?" Joey grinned. He aimed his camera at the dead man and took several photos.

"Talk about being in the right place at the right time," James remarked.

"Have we ruled him out of the Sally Nolan situation?" Robert asked.

"There was no evidence to suggest that he even saw her," James reminded him. "All we've got is that witness saying he saw him outside the house."

"And what was that witness doing, pray tell?"

"Walking his dog apparently," James replied.

Joey's camera started to flash again after he had moved into a different position.

"Mr Photographer of the Year," Robert said snidely. "It's a wonder our lady editor isn't here too."

"She is," James informed him.

"What? You're joking, aren't you?"

James pointed to the long table. "She's over there."

143

Robert swung round to see Maggie Lehane with a glass in hand. She appeared to be deep in conversation with a tall pale-faced gentleman.

"Strange all these murders have started happening since she came to town," Robert said. He fixed his eyes on Maggie. She was wearing a dark suit with a white blouse that looked as if it had been bleached to within an inch of its life. She looked really good, if he cared to admit it.

"This sleepy little town seems to be waking up," James said with a grin.

"Yes, it sure is, and there'd be a lot less trouble if it gave one big yawn and put its bloody head back down on the pillow again," Robert quipped.

James Sayder was still smiling when Robert had managed to tear his eyes away from Maggie.

"What is your problem?" Robert snapped.

"If you don't mind me asking, sir."

"Yes."

"What's yours?"

Robert didn't answer; instead he reached out and grabbed Joey Tyrell roughly by the shoulder.

"Get out of here before I arrest you for contaminating a crime scene," Robert growled.

Joey moved off towards the long table.

Robert took his mobile phone from his inside pocket, and dialled the station's number.

"Another one down," he told the desk sergeant.

CHAPTER 34

"This is getting to be a bit like *Groundhog Day*," Dr Morris announced.

Robert stared grimly at the remains of the latest victim. "So, what's the story?" he asked.

Dr Morris tossed an extremely sharp-looking implement into a silver basin. "Same knife wound, same killer," Dr Morris replied.

"No point in pretending it isn't happening. We have a serial killer." Robert sighed.

The body of Dr Curtin looked so small on the gurney, like that of a child really, not a fully-grown adult. "I would have really liked to have had a word with him," Robert said.

Dr Morris straightened up before saying, "Maybe that's the reason why he was killed: to prevent him from talking to you."

"But who'd know that you were going to introduce him to me?" Robert asked.

"Not wishing to sound smart, but the killer knew," James Sayder interjected.

"Would he have known the judge personally?" Robert pointed to the body.

"I know I live here, but the way I'm all over the country with my job, I don't know what's going on here half the time," Dr Morris said.

"I'm trying to work out a connection between Dr Curtin here and Judge Mangan," Robert said.

"They would have met when Green Park was being sold," Dr Morris said. "Yes, of course, they would have had to sign things, and make mutual agreements."

"I don't get it," Robert said.

"The judge bought Green Park from Dr Curtin."

"Did he?"

"You did know that, didn't you?"

"How would I?"

"No, what I should have said was did you know Green Park was the mental institution that Dr Curtin ran? Except it was called Renovatio then. Judge Mangan changed the name after he bought it."

"Renovatio, what kind of a name is that?" Robert asked.

"It's Latin, it means renewal." Dr Morris laughed. "I just knew all that Latin I had to learn would come in handy one day."

"So how long ago did all that business come about then?" Robert asked.

"1995 if I remember rightly. There was a lot of speculation going on at the time. The place cost a fortune, and you know the way people think. 'There must be money in judging' was the favourite phrase kicking about."

"And is there money in judging?" Robert asked.

"Old Mangan was rotten with money anyway: the old la-di-dah set, old money, as they say."

"Lucky old him," Robert said.

"Anyway, back to our man here," Dr Morris said in a business-like fashion.

Robert turned his attention back to the gurney. "Poor sod," he remarked.

"He was so excited about this psychology book he was writing, and look at him now," Dr Morris said.

"We'll have to look through that manuscript, or whatever you call it," Robert told James. "There might be clues in it."

"Work in progress, sir, and yes, you are right, there could be useful information in it."

"Tell me, Dr Morris, did you happen to notice that hoodie chap hanging around before you left our man here?" Robert asked.

"Afraid I didn't."

"The hoodie could have been a woman," James offered.

"True."

"Women are more into poisoning," Dr Morris said. "Not my theory though, I used it in a thesis I was doing one time."

"Pity there aren't CCTV cameras in Cliff's," James said.

"That's why the killer felt so safe," Doctor Morris suggested.

"Why kill him in the restaurant though?" Robert asked.

"Because he or she is extremely confident," James replied.

"Or else he or she wanted an audience," Robert stated. "The killer wanted the whole funeral party to become aware of the daring act that was carried out right under their noses."

"Or else it was us, and us alone, the killer was aiming at. We were the audience he wanted to witness his daring act. He's playing with us, sir," James said. "He is laughing at us."

"Don't forget the she," Robert quipped.

"Speaking of shes, wasn't it handy our illustrious editor and her photographer happened to be present?" James said knowingly.

Robert picked up on the statement. "As I keep saying, nothing but murder since she restarted that rag of a newspaper."

"Have you got her down as a suspect?" Dr Morris inquired.

"At this stage, everyone's a suspect," Robert said gruffly.

"That is, everyone in possession of a dark-coloured hoodie," James said, half in jest.

Robert laughed. "Well, that narrows it down considerably."

"There's something bothering me," Dr Morris said.

"What?" Robert asked.

"The doctor here had a briefcase laid down on the seat beside him when we were talking. I presumed it contained the manuscript, or work-in-progress of his theories as you quite rightly pointed out, James. You remember I was telling you that he asked me to have a look at his work? He planned to bring it along on the day of the funeral."

"I don't, actually, but knowing me my mind was probably elsewhere," Robert said.

"Have you people got it?"

"What?"

"The briefcase, it was a brown leather affair."

"Might have got overlooked," Robert reasoned. "We'll check it out, it's probably somewhere in the restaurant. More than likely it got kicked under a table during all the mayhem."

Dr Morris removed his plastic gloves and binned them. "Right, that's it for now."

Robert turned to go.

Dr Morris directed his gaze at James. "Nice young lady you had with you in the Cornerstone last night," he said.

Robert swung round.

"I've seen her around; she's a nurse, isn't she?" the doctor continued.

"Yes, she's working up in Mary I's," James said sheepishly.

Robert looked James in the face. The young man was blushing like mad.

"A nurse?" Robert smiled. "What happened to the receptionist?"

James laughed trying to hide his embarrassment.

"Working your way through the professions, are you?" Robert teased.

"That's right I am," James replied. Quickly he turned on his heel and made his way to the exit, praying that no one had noticed his burning face.

Lucky devil, Robert thought inwardly as he followed him outside.

CHAPTER 35

"This must be the most isolated place in the whole universe," Robert said.

"And we'd never have found it if not for our desk sergeant, who is in my opinion a fountain of knowledge," James replied.

"The good old sergeant was stationed in that town we passed earlier on, and thanks to the stint he did there, he knows every out-of-the-way place around here. This area is called Green Vale by the way, and you won't find it on those Googlemaps for all their so-called technology," Robert said.

The inside of Dr Curtin's house was as dreary as the outside. Books and papers were placed at strategic points, like some form of eccentric filing.

After much searching, Robert located what appeared to be a record of the Renovatio patients written in a black hard-backed journal.

"Here, James, you take charge of that. In fact, you might go through it in your spare time, you're much better at figuring things out than I am."

"There's no sign of a manuscript or anything like it, wouldn't you think he'd have a copy of it here for safekeeping?" James remarked.

"Look at all this handwritten stuff, it must have taken him years to produce this, had he intended typing it, I wonder." Robert pointed in the direction of the grey Brother typewriter on a desk by the window.

"He doesn't have a computer, isn't that strange? Everyone's got one nowadays," James reasoned.

"He grew up in the typewriter age and most of those old dinosaurs just don't change with the times," Robert said.

"But you'd be surprised at the old dinosaurs who are up-to-date with all the latest tech stuff."

"Do you know what's puzzling me?" Robert said.

"What?"

"Why wasn't he killed here?"

"The killer might not have known where he lived? Or else our killer did know but wanted a public execution, punishment for all to see – like we were saying in Cliff's, sir," James reasoned.

"The judge and Miss Nolan's killings were done in private, but now he's gone up a notch with a public execution. Why?"

"Execution, punishment, let's go with that theory," James suggested.

"But for what were they being punished? What had all three of them done that was so bad?" Robert asked.

"The briefcase seems to have vanished into thin air, sir. What was in it that was so important?"

"It's obvious that the briefcase was what the killer was after, and he killed the doctor for whatever damning information it harboured."

Carefully James pulled out a drawer. "I wonder if Miss Lehane knows anything about that briefcase," he said.

"You can bet your sweet bippy there's going to be another front-page story pretty soon," Robert replied.

The drawer revealed nothing of interest, prompting James to move towards the bookcase by the door.

James laughed. "Sweet bippy, sir?"

"There was an American show in the sixties, 'Rowan & Martin's Laugh-In'. They used that phrase all the time."

James smiled. "Before your time, sir."

"They were doing reruns for years," Robert explained.

"The musty smell in here is stifling. Did the good doctor ever open a window?" James said. "I'll get a sneezing fit in a minute."

Robert waved a sheet of paper in the air. "Oh, look at this, will you? It's the eulogy that Dr Curtin gave at the funeral. He must have learned it by heart because I didn't see him referring to any notes," Robert said.

James picked up a framed photo which was sitting alone on the top shelf of the bookcase. "According to his little speech, he and the judge were the best of buddies."

"Our learned friend, Dr Morris, didn't give that impression, did he?" Robert remarked.

"He did say he didn't know what was going on half the time."

"So, the killer was probably in the church, listening to the compliments being spouted out. Compliments he didn't agree with. Couldn't you just imagine him getting angrier by the minute, and having to patiently wait to carry out his plan?" Robert said.

"It was a great plan, so great we were caught rotten," James said as he approached Robert.

"What have you there?"

"Take a look, sir."

Robert studied the photo of the three people obviously on holiday from the looks of their swimwear garb. The woman stood in the middle smiling like a Cheshire cat. Her two companions, one wearing sunglasses, seemed in equally good form. They were all tanned and healthy-looking against the deep blue sea which was plainly visible in the background.

"They weren't in this country, that's for sure," James said.

"Some nice exotic island by the looks of it. So, who are these young holidaymakers?"

"The woman could be Miss Sally Nolan."

"You could be right. That gummy mouth is a dead giveaway. There was a photo in her house that looked like this one."

"It was a copy of this very photo. I'd lay my life on it," James said.

"Well done, James."

"One of the men has to be Dr Curtin. Why else would he have the photo?" James reasoned.

"This guy here, he looks remarkably like a young Judge Mangan."

"You're right, sir, they were buddies as we deduced from the eulogy. But Miss Sally Nolan, on holiday with them, why do you think that was?"

"We know Sally Nolan worked for Mangan, so that's the connection there, isn't it?"

"Yes, but what I meant was—"

"Come on, James, spit it out."

"I think one of them was... was... um... ah," James struggled to find a suitable word.

"Her lover. Dr Morris did say she had a child." Robert said.

"Yes, her lover," James said.

Robert remembered the doctor's quip about brown paper bags. "So which one of them had to have a constant supply?"

CHAPTER 36

James Sayder was wearing his hair loose and it was gleaming in the morning sun.

Robert was on the verge of asking James if he'd just shampooed it, but changed his mind. Firstly because it sounded gay, and secondly because James might think he was alluding to something about his gender, and he didn't want to go upsetting things now that he'd developed a bit of rapport with him.

James was clever and full of the enthusiasm that Robert had lacked when he was his age, although he did have his moments. It hadn't been all doom and gloom.

So, how was he functioning nowadays? That was the question he pondered. He had got into a rut, too tired to bother getting overexcited about anything.

But, much to his surprise, even if he was reluctant to admit it, for the past few mornings he'd woken up with a slight tinge of excitement bubbling inside him.

There seemed to be an extra spring in James's step too, Robert noted, turning his attention back to the young man walking beside him. The bagging of the nurse was probably the reason for that, he assumed, yet here he was himself, living like a monk. Not that it weighed too heavily on his mind, he had grown used to the celibate life now.

"I've checked out the list of Renovatio inmates," James reported.

"And?"

"Two of them with a local connection are still alive and well," James said.

"They are hardly living here though."

"Yes, they're here in Magnerstown."

"Are they really?"

"One is actually working for, believe it or not, *The Crier* newspaper," James said.

"This is good stuff," Robert said gleefully. The thought of having one up on Maggie Lehane lightened his mood considerably.

"He was a patient in Renovatio for a few months it seems."

"So, is it the beardy photographer then?"

"No, it's Mossie Harrington the compositor or typesetter, whatever they call themselves nowadays."

"And the other person?"

"A lady who happens to be a patient in Mary I's. Her name is Mary Hammond."

"Oh yes, Mary I's, where your young lady nurses."

"Sister Mary Immaculate's Nursing Home to give it its full title."

"Good work, James. We'll see what these two are going to have to say for themselves, shall we?"

"I'm afraid we're going to have no luck with the lady though."

"Why?"

"She's an invalid; I imagine she must have had a stroke, the poor woman, so her speech is hugely affected."

"Don't tell me she won't be able to talk to us," Robert said.

"Exactly, she can't communicate at all."

"One of the living dead, eh?" Robert said sympathetically. "So, Renovatio didn't live up to its promise. No renewal for her."

"Sorry, sir, but that's the story."

"Pity."

"Will we bring him in, sir, this Mossie Harrington chappie?"

"All these happenings are keeping Mr Harrington in a job. He could have had a motive for the killing of the good Dr Curtin, because of something that happened in Renovatio perhaps."

"You could be right about that," James said.

"And the other two deaths, could he be connected to them as well?"

"Possibly," James replied.

"Our esteemed editor never filled me in on her sources of information, you know?" Robert said.

"Is she getting inside information do you think?"

"From him, Mossie Harrington, you mean? You couldn't get more inside than that now, could you?"

"From the horse's mouth, so to speak."

"Speaking of which, your young lady could be our horse's mouth."

"Her name is Katie Manning," James related. "But she doesn't look at all like a horse," he added.

"Am I right in thinking it was your Katie who gave you the information about Mary Hammond's present health condition?"

"Yes."

"Maybe you could get her to find out a few more things," Robert suggested.

"You mean she could be our insider?" James asked.

"Yes, and there's nothing like a bit of inside information, wouldn't you agree?"

James smiled broadly as he opened the door of Dunworth's pub. Robert tapped his stomach as he slipped

156

inside. "I'm having a full Irish because I'm absolutely starving this morning," he said.

"Just coffee for me, sir, I've already had breakfast."

"Up early were you, James?"

"Yes, I had a bit of catch-up to do; I hate letting things slide, you see?"

Robert pulled a chair out and sat down. "I used to be a morning person myself once, but nowadays I'm built for comfort, not for speed," he said.

James smiled politely at the approaching waitress. Turning his attention back to Robert he said, "Nothing wrong with a bit of comfort, sir."

CHAPTER 37

Robert studied the man sitting opposite him. "Where were you on Monday between noon and one o'clock?" he asked.

"At home having lunch."

"Any witnesses?"

"Yes."

"Who?"

"Sparky."

Robert picked up a pen and prepared to write. "Surname and address please," he said.

"Address is the same as mine and as for a surname, now that's a tricky one, would your dog have the same surname as yourself?"

"Are you trying to be smart?" Roberts snarled.

"Just stating the facts."

"Did you know Dr Curtin?"

"Why?"

Robert threw the pen back onto the desk. "Just curious," he said.

"Think I killed him, do you?"

"I didn't say that did I?"

"I knew him years ago," Mossie offered. "You probably know that anyway."

"You were a patient in Renovatio," Robert prompted.

"Yeah I was," Mossie said contemptuously.

"So how did you get on with the good doctor while you were there?"

"I didn't get on with him at all because he was the bollix of all bollixes," Mossie said.

"So you didn't like him?"

Mossie quickly calmed down. Inwardly he warned himself not to lose it with these fellows, or he'd be here all night, a prospect he didn't relish.

"So why were you in Renovatio?" Robert continued.

"I was depressed."

"A little more than that, surely," Robert said.

Mossie made no reply.

Robert took a different approach. "You were put in there, weren't you?" he said.

"Yes," Mossie answered.

"Do you want to tell us about it?"

"I'm sure you know the whole story," Mossie snapped. "You have all the gory details in your dinosaur department, haven't you?"

"Yes, but we'd like to hear it from you."

"I was drunk and disorderly, that's the legal term for it, I do believe," Mossie said grudgingly.

"There was more to it than that, surely?" Robert asked.

"I wrecked the pub, is that what you want to hear me say?"

"Which is why you were committed," Robert suggested, leaving out the mental institution bit. Elaboration wasn't necessary; the man knew what he was referring to. There was no need to act the prick and rub his nose in it.

Mossie struggled to gain control. He was hot and sweaty. There was no window in the interview room, no air. It reminded him of that room which was no more than a cell, in the nut house with the fancy name Renovatio.

Even to this day, he'd sometimes wake up in the middle of the night, and for a split second he'd think he was back there. All those injections he'd been given can't have been good. They were bound to have left a mark, bound to have been the cause of the nightmares he sometimes had.

"So, tell us about Judge Mangan," Robert said.

"What about him?"

"You didn't like him either, did you?"

"What do you think?"

"Why don't you indulge us?" Robert nodded in James's direction to acknowledge the 'us'.

"I was up before him for drunk driving," Mossie said.

"And in your opinion he was a bit hard on you, which would be why you've resented him all these years."

Mossie smiled. "I can't afford resentments. That's what my sponsor in AA was always trying to drum into my thick head."

"I'd imagine you didn't shed any tears when you heard the judge had been murdered," Robert stated.

Mossie rose to the bait, "He put a terrible strain on me and my wife with his so-called punishment-to-fit-the-crime shit, and the same bollix driving around half-scuttered all the time. We didn't see you lot doing anything about that, did we?"

"You must have really hated it when you found yourself up before him again in court after the pub fracas. You must have really flipped when he ordered you into that mental place." Robert decided it was time for nose rubbing, deliberately injecting 'mental place' in the hope it would make Mossie mad enough to rattle off more.

"He colluded with that other bollix, Curtin, great friends the two of them were. The judge ordered that I be put into that place, another customer for Dr Frankenstein. Curtin was using drugs on people which hadn't been tested out on humans."

"That's a serious accusation," Robert remarked.

"Think it isn't true, do you?"

"So, how did you feel when you heard the judge was dead?"

"Want the truth?"

"Yes, please," Robert replied.

"I laughed my arse off," Mossie said. "I was on a euphoric high and it didn't cost me a penny."

"Let me get this straight, you admit you hated the judge, and Dr Curtin, and they both end up dead."

"Great, isn't it?" Mossie said gleefully. "Two birds killed with one stone."

"Do you by any chance own a dark-coloured hooded fleece?" Robert asked.

Before Mossie had a chance to reply, the door opened and the desk sergeant poked his head in.

Robert was annoyed with the interruption. "What is it?" he asked.

"The editor of *The Crier* is on the blower. She wants to know when you'll be finished with her man. There's a paper to be printed, she says."

"Is there now?" Robert said sarcastically.

"And there's a solicitor outside, says she sent him here to represent Mr Harrington."

"Hasn't she been a busy little bee?" Robert stood up. He knew he'd get no further now with this intervention.

"This interview is over," Robert announced. "For now, that is. Don't leave town, will you, Mr Harrington? You know the score."

"Think you're Magnum P.I., do you?" Mossie rose to his feet.

Robert shot him a warning look. "I'd keep my lip buttoned if I were you," he said.

Mossie Harrington sighed with relief once he found himself outside in the bracing air. He'd been stuck in that pokey little interview room for a whole hour before Magnum P.I. and son appeared on the scene.

Did they have some kind of two-way mirror and a profiler studying him like you see on television? he wondered. No, of course not. That would be a little farfetched for this backward town; they wouldn't know what to do with modern technology. Magnerstown was still a member of the flat-Earth society.

"Back to reality," Mossie said aloud as he hurried down the steps of the station. The plan was as follows: home to feed Sparky, a quick bite to eat and back to *The Crier*. After all, there was – as Maggie had quite rightly said – a paper to be got out. But the first thing he'd have to do the minute he got home was to get rid of his hooded fleece. Burning the thing would be the only way of making sure it wouldn't be found by Magnum P.I. and son.

CHAPTER 38

James Sayder dreaded the thought of spending an evening at his uncle's house. He'd been invited to dinner, which was to be cooked by the perfect wife and host Helen.

He did not like the lovely Helen, and neither did his mother; in fact, she once told him if she had to sit for more than ten minutes in the same room as the snobby Helen, she would gladly commit *harakiri* just to get away from her.

As he seated himself at the table, James couldn't help wondering why he'd been afforded the invitation, and the only explanation he could come up with was that it was a fact-finding mission on his uncle's behalf.

"So, how are you getting on, James? Our small town must be boring you to death after city life," Helen began the inquisition.

"No, actually I'm enjoying it here," James replied.

"I believe so," Helen's voice had an element of sardonic amusement in it, and it was enough to set off alarm bells in James' head.

Was she hinting at Katie? Had she found out something? Of course she had – James resigned himself to the possibility that some yapper at the hairdresser's had spilled the beans.

News travelled fast in this town, faster than email even.

A bowl of steaming hot soup was put down in front of James by a young Polish girl whose name was Maria.

James knew all about Maria, he'd heard his uncle praising the girl at the station, saying how lucky Helen and himself had been to procure her. It seemed this young woman was measuring up to Helen's standards, a mammoth achievement indeed.

Helen stared directly into James's eyes when Maria stepped out of the way. "So, tell us about your young woman," she said.

James swallowed hard and busied himself by breaking the roll, and laying it out in pieces on the side plate that was so shiny, he could see the blur of his reflection in it.

"Her name's Katie Manning, but we're just friends," James spluttered. He hadn't expected to be explaining his own actions.

"She works in St. Mary Immaculate's." Helen confirmed she knew all about Katie.

"Yes, she's a nurse," James replied.

"It's not serious though, is it?" James's uncle interjected. James was surprised that the man had actually opened his mouth without prior permission from his wife.

"Your mother would surely expect you to do a smidge better than that, or doesn't she care?" Helen ignored her husband with the contempt she thought he deserved. She also ignored the fact that James had a father who kept in touch with his son.

James knew Helen was a glorified snob, but tonight she was surpassing herself.

"Nursing is a profession that's highly overrated." Helen was on a roll. "Glorified domestics is all they are, emptying bedpans and what have you."

James froze, he wanted to stand up and walk out, but he couldn't risk upsetting the cow, because he knew she'd be on the phone to his mother with gross exaggerations. This would result in his time in Magnerstown coming to an abrupt end, because his mother wouldn't be able to resist telling Helen to fuck off. Helen had always tried to make her feel like a second-class citizen just because she was husbandless. It was Helen's opinion that a woman who couldn't hold onto her man was severely deficient.

"They're a bit common, aren't they? The Mannings." Helen was not letting up.

Lucky for James, Maria interrupted as she returned to collect the soup bowls. He was finding it hard to contain himself.

The word 'common' echoed in James's head. He hadn't met Katie's family yet, but she'd told him all about them. They lived on their small farm holding halfway between Magnerstown and Vitalstown. Even though they worked hard, according to Katie the result didn't produce enough earnings for them to survive on, which meant the Social Welfare payments were a necessity to keep food on the table.

"So how are you faring out with Robert Carroll?" was the next question asked.

James eyed the plate that had been set down in front of him by the dutiful Maria.

"It's venison," Helen informed him.

He knew that. Did she think he was some kind of moron? It was the blood oozing out of it that had caught his attention. One thing he hated was half-cooked meat, even if it was supposed to be good.

Maria was smiling down at him, a bowl of mixed vegetables in one hand, spoon in the other.

"Vegetables," she offered.

James nodded.

"So how is Robert Carroll behaving himself?" Helen asked.

"I like him," James replied. Quickly, he turned his attention back to his food because the smarmy look on her face was annoying him so much he wanted to throw something at her, preferably the live thing on his plate. What label did she have for Robert?

"He made a right mess of things with that beautiful French girlfriend of his," Helen said.

James felt his throat tightening, if he didn't get out of here soon, he'd swing for her.

"How's the case going?" James's uncle got in with a question.

"Everything's coming along well," James answered.

"I expect Robert is dragging his heels as usual," Helen sneered.

James was adamant that he was not going to get sucked into this line of critique of Robert and concentrated on the lump of meat on his plate. He cut a small piece off and, as the blood oozed out of it, Judge Mangan's throat came to mind.

CHAPTER 39

Greg was so engrossed in the business of organizing the photographs he had laid out that he didn't hear the tapping on the campervan door.

"Hello, anyone there?"

The voice made his heart leap momentarily. Gathering himself, he scooped up the pictures, tucked them under a newspaper and shouted out, "Coming."

James Sayder got straight to the point, "I'd like to ask you some questions."

"Howzit," Greg smiled.

"Can I come in?" James asked.

"'Fraid not," Greg replied. Nobody was getting into his van. He knew everything was in order inside, there was nothing on show to connect him to anything untoward, he'd made sure of that, but still he couldn't risk this potential nosey parker having a gander.

"I'm a police officer," James said, giving himself a promotion.

"You still can't come in," Greg said. "I've got company if you see what I mean."

"But I do need to talk to you, it's extremely important."

"Can talk to you later though, I'll drop by around seven o'clock," Greg said.

"See you at the station so," James agreed.

"Ya, see you there then."

"Know where it is, do you?"

"Sure do."

James handed Greg a card with his mobile number written on it. "Ring me beforehand to confirm you're coming and I'll meet you there."

"Ya, will do."

"Oh, and one other thing, you might bring your passport with you."

Greg smiled. "Passport, eh? You afraid I'm an illegal alien?"

"Just formality," James explained. "You do have one, don't you?"

"Ya wouldn't get too far without one, eh?"

"See you later so."

James departed and Greg hurried back into the van, he had to plan his strategy. The first and most important chore he'd have to attend to was to get rid of that briefcase and its contents, which in his opinion was the greatest heap of rubbish he'd ever read. It only went to confirm his belief that Dr Curtin was indeed off his rocker.

CHAPTER 40

James and Robert sat opposite Greg in the station interview room.

James introduced Robert and sat back in his chair giving him the lead-in.

Robert studied the passport Greg had furnished.

"So, tell us, what you are doing in this country? You're not Irish, are you?" Robert began.

"I was actually born here in Magnerstown, but I was sent to Cape Town to foster parents," Greg explained. "They eventually adopted me though."

"Your mother wasn't married," James interjected. "Mary Hammond, your real mother that is."

"Is that a crime?" Greg laughed.

Robert took over. "No, course not, just wondering if maybe she couldn't cope with having no support when you were born, if you get my meaning."

"Ya, I get your meaning," Greg said.

"She spent some time in Renovatio, the um... the... um," Robert searched for a word that wasn't too offensive.

Greg laid the palms of his hands down on the desk. "Looney bin," he said.

"I wouldn't go that far." Robert was embarrassed by Greg's forthrightness.

"Let's call a spade a spade," Greg said. "It was a place for people with mental issues."

"Can you tell us a bit about yourself?" Robert asked.

"What do you want to know?"

"Always best to start at the beginning," James said softly.

"As I told ya, I ended up in Cape Town with the Jouberts."

"Are the Jouberts related to your mother?"

"No."

"So some adoption agency had you shipped off to Cape Town, which is as good a destination as any I suppose," Robert stated.

"Cape Town, the Mother City, you couldn't get better than that," Greg replied.

"But why did you wait until now to come visit your mother?"

"You know what it's like, you get to a point in your life when you get a bit soft," Greg explained.

"You've got there quickly so, seeing you're only twenty-eight," Robert said.

"I'm old before my time," Greg replied.

"Did you have much trouble tracing her, your real mother I mean?"

"In this town?" Greg scoffed.

"Yeah, just stand on the main street and shout out the name," Robert agreed.

"Did you ever meet Dr Curtin?"

"Who?"

"The man who was in charge of Renovatio," Robert said.

"The geezer who got himself killed?" Greg deliberated.

"Yes."

"No."

"So, what are your plans for the future? Are you going to stay around for a while?" Robert asked.

"Ya, I was thinking along those lines."

"I'm sorry about your mother, can't be easy for you."

"At least she's still alive," Greg replied.

Robert rose to his feet and went and opened the door. "Right, we'll see you around so," he said.

"What about my passport? You holding it?"

"No, you can take it," Robert answered.

James pushed the passport across the desk to Greg.

As soon as Greg departed, Robert returned to the desk.

"What do you think of him?" James asked.

"He seems a nice enough fellow," Robert answered.

"I'm not so sure, something odd about him. I have this sort of sixth sense thing that makes me feel uncomfortable around some people. You'll think I'm like an old woman now."

"A sixth sense, eh? That's not a bad thing to have. We will have to keep our eye on him then. A sixth sense should never be ignored, James. Always trust the gut, that's what I say."

CHAPTER 41

Maggie pulled the zip of her new pink fleece all the way down; she was beginning to heat up, and it wasn't the brisk walking that was making her blood boil – it was thinking about Robert Carroll and his antics that was causing her such aggravation.

Poor Mossie was doing his best with his life, and that blithering idiot pulls him in for questioning. Was he so desperate to pin the murders on someone that he had to pick on Mossie of all people? Mossie wouldn't harm a fly, of that she was certain. And worse still, did Mr Plod not realize he was messing with someone's sobriety?

Anyway, the paper is ready to go now and Mossie has gone off to his AA meeting.

She was pleased with herself for keeping up the walking regime, and glad she hadn't abandoned it like some of her other objectives; like the gardening, for instance. She would have to get someone to come and sort it out for her once and for all, after that she'd offer to pay them a few euro every time they came to do a couple hours of work. She made a mental note to take a good look at the notice board in the supermarket which she'd only briefly glanced at up to now. There was bound to be some handyman looking for casual work among the array of handwritten and typewritten cards. That was something *The Crier* could offer too, situations vacant and services offered columns, she mused. She could discuss it with the lads to see what they thought; she valued Mossie and Joey's input. They made a great team, the three of them.

Joey Tyrell had got an old photos thing going. He'd invited readers to send in their yesteryear photos to the 'Where Are They Now?' feature he'd created, and there was great positive feedback coming in about the venture.

Mossie had got his vet friend to do a column on the care of pets, and that had attracted hordes of readers' questions.

The Crier was selling well in the town and surrounding areas at the moment, the murders were helping things immensely, but somehow she knew the paper would continue to flourish even without the macabre happenings.

People did like having a local weekly paper, because Magnerstown never ever got a mention in the nationals – it was like the place wasn't on the map at all.

True, the murders had got a mention in the leading papers, but they got it all wrong. They hadn't even bothered coming to check it out.

Yes, there was no doubt about it – *The Crier* was well streamlined now, and she could sit back and wallow in its success.

Gradually she increased her pace; her fitness level had improved immensely. Overall she was feeling the benefits of her new lifestyle, her skin was looking clear and clean, she'd cut down on the makeup because she didn't need it, just a quick application of moisturizer cream and lip gloss made her look good. It was with great satisfaction that she realized for the first time in years, she was actually happy in mind and body thanks to her new job and a more casual lifestyle.

The sight of Robert Carroll made her stop short.

He had gotten out of a car and was making his way to his front door after waving off the driver. She knew it would have been someone from the station dropping him off. Mossie had told her Mr Plod didn't own a car, and he'd never seen him even driving a cop car. She wondered about that: could he drive at all? Maybe she'd ask him to fill her in. Or maybe she just wouldn't bother.

Her annoyance with his arrogance came back to the surface as she stood there watching him search his pockets for his keys, the bungling idiot.

He hadn't noticed her, she knew, so she continued to watch as he slipped inside the house and slammed his front door shut.

He couldn't close it like an ordinary person, the clumsy oaf. He was like a big fat bull in a china shop. Only he wasn't fat, he had quite a sporty physique. Fit. Fit to drop, she laughed.

It was just starting to get dark. She loved this time of the day when nature turned down the light.

She could appreciate all these things now that she was away from city living, she certainly didn't miss the rat race and all that went with it.

As she drew level with Robert's front door she had an incredible urge to bawl him out for his treatment of Mossie, and without giving it another thought she hammered on the institutional grey door.

Robert couldn't hide his surprise at the sight of her standing on his doorstep.

"You absolute prick." She thumped him on the chest.

He caught her by the wrists to prevent a repeat performance, and with their faces extremely close, he gritted his teeth and looked her right in the eye.

He could feel her chest rising and falling she was that close, and the smell of her sweat was almost sweet, but he could see the contempt she was feeling for him written all over her face.

"What's wrong with you?" he asked.

Maggie was calming down now that she'd vented her spite by giving him a good thump.

Robert didn't relax his grip on her because he wasn't certain it was safe to do so.

"I was bang out of order there," Maggie whispered.

He let go of her wrists; she stepped back a few paces.

"I am really feeling a lot better now, because I wanted to whack you for a while now," Maggie laughed.

"I'm glad I could be of assistance, Miss Lehane."

"So tell me, Mr Plod, are you going to arrest me for assault?" she asked.

He knew she was making fun of him and he didn't rise to the bait.

"You're an arrogant sod and I'll have to think of some other way to punish you," she said with a grin.

Maggie broke into a trot. She was anxious to get back to Forge Cottage to chill out with a large glass of wine and a good wallow in the knowledge that Robert Carroll fancied her big time.

It felt so good to have that kind of power over the policeman and, by God, she was really enjoying it.

For one split second, she admitted the anticipation bubbling up inside her was roaring to be sated immediately if not sooner, but she would control the situation.

She was not going to allow desire to pull her into submission, not just yet.

She'd draw the whole thing out for as long as she could. After all, it was a well-known fact that the chase is better than the catch. She'd change all that though, she'd make the catch as good the chase.

She laughed out loud as she conjured up the image of Robert Carroll in the guise of a lapdog begging on his knees, for a juicy titbit from her table.

She laughed out loud. *You are good, Maggie Lehane.*

CHAPTER 42

Katie Manning fitted herself neatly into the passenger seat of James Sayder's car and placed her tiny white handbag on the dashboard.

James bent forward and kissed her cheek.

"You old charmer you," Katie gushed.

James's attention turned to the man who was emerging from the entrance door of Mary I's Nursing Home. It had begun to rain and the man who was wearing a dark fleece jacket, pulled the hood up.

"Who's he?" James asked.

"Are you ever off duty?"

James continued to study the man who was now approaching the car.

"I reckon he's going to have a good look at us," he said.

Katie grabbed her handbag and pretended to be looking for something in it.

James felt a sense of foreboding as he realized who the voyeur was when he walked past.

"His name is Greg Joubert," James confirmed. "We interviewed him at the station."

"Was it in connection with the killings?" Katie asked.

"It was good of you to give me the information about Mary Hammond, but now I have another favour to ask."

"You want me to tell you what I know about him," Katie said. "All I can tell you is he turned up a few weeks ago, claiming to be Mary Hammond's long-lost son."

"He's a bit weird, don't you think?" James remarked.

Katie returned her handbag to the dashboard.

"I agree, there's something strange about him alright, and the way he talks, sometimes he says the oddest kind of things."

"It's the lingo they use in Cape Town, that's where he comes from," James explained.

"So, that's the reason his skin is so tanned."

"Does Mary Hammond have any other relatives visit her?"

"No – only him, and he comes to see her every day, sometimes twice even, and he's always bringing her things, like presents and stuff. The other day he brought her a handkerchief, which I thought was a bit peculiar to be honest about it."

"So you'd be on speaking terms with him," James said.

"If I didn't know you were a cop I'd think you were jealous." Katie threw her head back and laughed. A strand of hair came undone from her topknot hairstyle, which she always wore when on duty.

James gently pushed the wayward strand behind her ear.

"You are the most caring fellow I have ever come across," Katie said.

"And you are the biggest giver of compliments I have ever come across," James replied.

Katie brought the conversation back to Greg Joubert. "He gives me the creeps, he does."

"Me too," James said.

"Shall I keep an eye on him, be your assistant? Like the way you are to Detective Inspector Robert Carroll, to give him his full title," Katie said.

"You could make his title fuller by adding grumpy. He's off the cigarettes, you see."

"My father gave up the cancer sticks three years ago, and he was unbearable for ages. My mother used to tell him when he started whinging and whining, that he sounded like a gnat having a vasectomy." Katie tapped James's shoulder playfully.

James's thoughts turned to Robert. He came across as a lonely sort of man, and there was definitely a look of envy on his face when he found out about his friendship with Katie.

"They say nicotine is worse than any drug." Katie broke in on his thoughts.

"Yes, poor Mr Carroll is having terrible withdrawal symptoms."

"Well, I hope he is successful in kicking the habit," Katie smiled. "Cigarettes aren't good for anybody's health."

"Oh he's pretty determined alright, I reckon he'll do it."

Katie reached for her handbag. "Well, I'd better be getting back to work then," she said.

"What was that you said about the handkerchief?"

"I said the handkerchief struck me as a bit peculiar, that's all."

"Why?"

"Well, her initial is M and his is G."

"And."

"D was the initial on the handkerchief."

"Just the one handkerchief he brought her, you said?"

"Yes, he could have taken it from a box set of handkerchiefs that he had himself, or he might have just got that one in a sale or something – you know the way they sell off odd stuff that's fallen out of packets," Katie reasoned.

"Be careful with that fellow," James advised.

"You bet I will."

"He's a dark horse, no doubt about it."

"Speaking of dark horses," Katie smiled.

"Yeees."

"Your lovely uncle."

"What about him?"

"No, forget it, I shouldn't be saying it."

"What?"

"It's none of my business really, but..." Katie trailed off.

"Come on, Katie, you have to tell me now that you've got me all interested," James said.

"I saw him the other night with somebody."

"Somebody?"

"A woman."

"Well, thank God for that, I thought you were going to say it was a man he was with," James joked.

"I'm trying to be serious here," Katie said.

"Sorry."

"They were looking very cosy together, as a matter of fact it was evident they are having a thing together if I may say so, but only to you I'm saying it, I'm not a gossip."

"Well, that rules his wife out so." James laughed. "She's colder than ice."

"I thought he'd be too straight-laced for that kind of thing seeing he's got such an important job and all, you'd think he'd be above board."

"Never underestimate a man, Katie," James warned.

"I wonder if his wife knows."

James laughed heartily.

"What's so funny?"

"The lovely Helen, she is so patronizing, you wouldn't believe it; she seems to get a kick out of putting people down. You might think I'm cruel but she is one person who deserves a massive kick up the backside, and I am so glad this has happened to her," James said.

"Well, in that case she's probably driven the man to stray away from the fold because of her horrible behaviour," Katie reasoned.

"You don't happen to know who the woman is."

"Do you really need to know that?"

James laughed. "Yes, because I might have to use it as evidence against him."

"The Polish girl who works for them, that's who his partner in crime is."

"The much-praised, dutiful Maria." James laughed at the irony of it.

"I have to tell you though, I did say it to my nursing friend, in the strictest of confidence you understand, and he said the whole town knew they were having an affair."

Katie kissed him lightly on the lips before leaving the car. "See you tonight," she said.

"Look forward to it," James called after her and waited until she had disappeared into the building before starting up the car and driving away.

He would have to phone his mother and share this breaking news with her. He looked left and right before pulling out onto the main road. Yes indeed, he knew his darling mammy was going to get some kick out of hearing the gory details. She would be laughing for days at the thought of it.

He could just imagine her pouring herself a celebratory drink and raising the glass in a toast to Helen's image in her mind's eye. He could even hear her announcing to the empty room, 'It couldn't happen to a nicer person.'

Karma, sweet karma. James laughed as he drove back to the station.

CHAPTER 43

Maggie was having a restless night; it had been terribly hot for days now.

"What time is it now?" Maggie wondered aloud as she peered at her alarm clock.

It was three-fifteen; a half-hour since she'd last checked. She'd been in bed since midnight and still hadn't dropped off, so it was time for drastic action to remedy the situation. She removed her nightclothes and kicked off the duvet. Pulling the fitted sheet off the mattress she slipped in under it. The coolness of the cotton against her skin was a welcome improvement, and after sinking back on her pillows she felt sure she'd sleep now. Yet, after more twisting and turning, she thought about getting up. A cold drink, or a cold shower maybe. Hot as she was, a cold shower was definitely a bit too extreme.

Another hour passed and still sleep was eluding her.

"This is it," she groaned as she eased herself out of bed. There was no point in just lying there getting more and more frustrated by the minute.

For a split second, she thought she was imagining things when she saw the figure standing at the foot of her bed.

"For God's sake," she gasped as she focused on the man's face.

Equally surprised, he turned and made a hasty retreat banging the front door behind him.

She grabbed her mobile phone, and with shaking hands she searched for Robert Carroll's mobile number. He'd insisted on giving it to her in case she came across some information, and she'd obliged and put the number into her contact list, telling herself at the time that she'd never be calling him.

But here she was now, dialling his number.

* * *

"Did he touch you?" was the first thing Robert asked. He was out of breath after running to Forge Cottage.

Maggie led him into the kitchen. "No, he didn't," she replied.

"Did you recognize him? Is he someone you know?"

"It all happened so quickly," Maggie answered. "Christ, I need a drink."

She found the whiskey bottle tucked away in one of the cupboards.

"I made a few hot toddies last week, great when you've got a cold," she said.

She placed two glasses on the worktop and started pouring generous measures.

"What was he after? Nothing appears to be disturbed," Robert said after looking around.

"Things have been going missing," Maggie admitted.

"Like what?"

"Perfume, talcum powder, you know, small things like that... and..."

"What?"

"A handkerchief."

"A handkerchief," Robert said incredulously.

Maggie smiled. "It was a souvenir I'd kept, in memory of my former life."

"It would help if you could put a face on this intruder," Robert said.

"Why don't you take that jacket off? You look like you're going to explode."

Robert obliged and draped the jacket over a chair. He was boiling alright, in more ways than one, if only she knew it. She was wearing a thin cotton dressing gown and he knew she had nothing on underneath. He distracted himself by busily opening the top buttons of his shirt.

Maggie took a large gulp out of her own glass, and then held out the other drink to Robert.

"I'm afraid it's not your favourite tipple," she said.

Robert took a small sip and tried to hide his lack of appreciation. Her standing so close to him, on the other hand, he greatly appreciated.

Maggie topped up her glass. "Oh, I feel better already," she said.

She realized Robert wasn't too keen on the offering with the little sips he was taking. She'd have to get a bottle of that cognac he liked so much for his future visits. She laughed at herself for the way her thought pattern was going, she'd have to give herself a good scolding for losing the run of herself, but she knew in her heart and soul it was time for Robert Carroll to become very relevant in her life, there was no point in putting it off any longer.

"So, what did he look like, this intruder? Can you describe him?" Robert broke in on her thoughts.

Maggie drained her glass and put it back on the counter.

"His face was not exactly white, it was tanned like, and the eyes, I've seen those eyes before."

"That's something anyway, I'm sure it will come to you." Robert sounded hopeful.

Maggie suddenly remembered. "It was that young man."

"What young man?"

"The man I bumped into the day I was coming out of Pattie Flowers' shop. He was the one who helped me put some stuff in the car. He was wearing a hoodie, but it didn't prevent me from seeing his face."

"So, who is he? Do you know his name?" Robert asked.

"I don't, I'm afraid; and I've never seen him since. At least I don't think I have, oh I don't know, maybe I have, I'm so confused."

"Don't worry about it now, try and get some sleep."

"I don't think there's any likelihood of that now." Maggie looked straight into his face. "But you look as if you could use some sleep," she said.

She was feeling a lot calmer thanks to Robert's presence, and the whiskey was playing its part too.

"It's not sleep I'm interested in," Robert admitted throwing caution to the wind. He was going to make a go for her, tell her how he felt about her. Why not? All she could do was slap his face. He'd be man enough to accept defeat and slink away quietly nursing his humiliation, and never ever would he put himself through the ordeal of approaching her again, he promised himself. His ham-handed attempt at making a pass would probably be front page news in *The Crier* but he could live with that.

Maggie smiled and took him by the hand. "I know exactly what you're interested in," she said.

Robert was stunned, because he had psyched himself up for a right tongue lashing.

Maggie took the glass out of his other hand and laid it down on the counter.

"Yes, I know exactly what you're interested in, and you my dear man are going to get it big time," she said.

CHAPTER 44

Toby Jackson tore open his wage packet, it was fatter than usual, but not with extra money. A letter folded over several times was the offender.

Toby lit a cigarette and unfolded the letter.

The sound of a car starting up outside caught his attention, it was the neighbours from across the road, they were off for their usual Saturday shopping trip. Toby smiled, that was good news for him because it meant he wouldn't have to be putting up with their kid and his ball-kicking.

The letter was not good news though; it informed Toby that his wages would be paid into his bank account from now onwards, and asked that he furnish the office with his account number and sort code details.

Toby groaned. He didn't have a bank account. What did he need one for when he had a mattress to put his spare cash under? His Bank of Mattress suited him just fine, not that he had much dough left over after his weekly spend.

The trouble was that he'd have to go into the flipping place and fill out countless forms in order to open an account. Well then, if that's what his employers wanted, they'd better give him time off from the job to do it on Monday.

The bank didn't open until half-past ten, closed at four, and the only time he could go in would be during his own lunch hour, which happened to be theirs too. Toby was well aware that they closed bang on time at one, having had a nasty experience some months back. He had wanted to cash a bonus cheque he'd got from an insurance policy he'd surrendered, and just as he got to the door of the bank with a minute to spare, the smart-arse McGrath wouldn't let him in.

'The clerks are entitled to their full lunch hour,' McGrath had said in a smarmy voice. Who did he think he was, acting as if he was the bank manager himself? He was forgetting, of course, that everyone knew his true job description was 'the gofer.' The fetch-and-carry man in other words, with his head up his hole. He was a lick-arse of the highest order, and he'd get an award for it if there was one to be had.

The sound of the front door opening broke in on Toby's thoughts.

He hadn't left the key in the lock, had he? What cheeky so-and-so was coming into his house without being asked?

"Give me the keys to Green Park," the hooded figure barked on entering the room.

Toby, recovering from his initial shock, asked, "What do you want them for?"

"None of your business."

"Do I know you?"

"Just get the keys." There was anger in the voice, the kind of anger that could have a nasty matching action to go with it if cooperation wasn't forthcoming.

Toby knew full well it was best to do as he was told to save himself getting a slap.

After pocketing the keys, the hoodie pulled the net curtain off the window.

"My curtain," Toby protested.

Years of dust motes rose from the net curtain as the hoodie busied himself tearing it into strips.

Toby didn't have to be a scientist to work out what the strips were for.

"Sit down," the visitor ordered.

There was no point in arguing. Toby knew he would have to cooperate if he didn't want to end up getting a thrashing and maybe choking on his own blood. There'd be no one around to save him, and who was going to miss him? No one, that's who. The boys at the betting shop were too preoccupied with their own stuff to notice he wasn't there, and as for the pub crowd, they would only think he'd changed his drinking habits – wasn't he always moaning about the price of the pint, and how he was thinking of buying a few slabs of beer at the German discount store and drinking at home instead? Him and his big motormouth.

He wouldn't be missed until Monday morning. But that didn't necessarily mean they'd come looking for him. *He could be sick,* they'd think. By then he would be well dead anyway.

After finishing binding and gagging Toby, the hoodie stuffed some spare strips into his pocket. They were needed for his next job.

Toby could see the smirk on the intruder's face as he dropped the front door key on the table.

"Far too trusting you are, man, leaving your door key under the yoke outside. You should be more careful, there are queer hawks about."

"Everyone does it," Toby said, but it came out sounding like something Donald Duck would say.

"Well thanks again, Key Man."

The voice was really familiar; that strange accent.

The sound of the back-door bolt being drawn back echoed through the house. Leaving that way to minimize the risk of being seen, the cute bastard had covered everything.

Toby could feel a panic attack coming on because the thing that was causing him the most pain was the fact that he was absolutely dying for a fag.

CHAPTER 45

Fr. Scully looked at his watch. It was just twelve o'clock which meant it was time to call it a day. He was really looking forward to the afternoon. There was an old black-and-white Spencer Tracy film on television and he was going to take the telephone off the hook, lock the door and give himself 'me time.'

He took the stole from round his neck and proceeded to roll it up. The sound of the confessional box door opening stopped him in his tracks. He'd been sitting on his own for the last hour and now suddenly there was a client. Why didn't he go while he had the chance?

He pulled back the curtain to acknowledge the person on the other side of the grid.

A soft male voice came back at him. "Bless me, Father, for I have sinned."

Fr. Scully forced himself to sound interested. "Welcome son," he said.

This was going to be another boring confession. The sins would be of the usual calibre, lying cheating or stealing. Sex with someone else's wife was one that seemed to have crept in of late. Funnily enough the female sinner seldom made an admission of having extra-marital sex, perhaps they felt the end justified the means.

He'd hurry this man along though, give him a short penance of three Hail Marys and then he could rush off and have that mug of tea he was suddenly dying for.

"I have committed murder," the confessor said simply – as if it was nothing spectacular.

Fr. Scully threw his eyes up to Heaven. Obviously a joker here, he thought, and it was not even April Fool's Day.

"Not just one murder though," the confessor continued.

Fr. Scully decided it was best to go along with the fellow until he tired of the game. "Oh, how many murders?" he asked.

"Three, Father."

"They say it gets easier as you go along," Fr. Scully jested.

"You're not taking me seriously, are you?"

"Of course I am."

"They had to be punished."

Fr. Scully fingered the pipe in his pocket.

"Are you listening to me?"

"Yes, my son, I am all ears."

"The first one was the most deserving of all. He used to continually force himself on my mother. I was the result of all that brutality, and still he went on with his debauchery after my birth. I tried to stop it when I was ten. I stabbed him in the hand with a nail, the biggest one I could find, but it didn't do much damage to his ugly paw. The bastard had me sent away then, but I've come back and I've sorted him out the right way this time."

"That's a terrible story," Fr. Scully said.

"The second person I had to deal with was that hard-hearted soulless woman. She knew what was going on in the house, and yet she stood idly by, and said nothing. She could have helped my mother but no, she wasn't going to do any such thing. Why? Because she was the bastard's old crony wasn't she, so she was hardly going to speak out against him—"

"And the third?" Fr. Scully interjected.

"The man who kept my mother prisoner in a place she shouldn't have been in. She was the victim and she was the one who got punished. She had medication funnelled into her until she became so stupefied that all she could do was shuffle around; she was so bad that she didn't even know her own name."

"Terrible." Fr. Scully hoped the word would suffice.

"A life wasted."

"Yes, indeed it was." The priest agreed, and if he didn't get a tea and tobacco fix soon he'd be committing murder himself.

"She's still no better off even though she's out of that place. For her, it's just a case of swapping one prison for another."

Silence followed.

"Is she in hospital?" Fr. Scully asked. He realized he'd have to speed things up or else he'd be here all day.

"A nursing home."

Fr. Scully reached out for the curtain. "Ah that's more comfortable for her I'm sure. Now is there anything else I can do for you?" he asked.

"Are you not shocked, Father? I murdered three people."

"God is merciful," Fr. Scully said. "I'm sure he has forgiven you already."

"You bless my mother every Sunday."

"Do I?"

"She can't even talk or walk, she's just like one of the living dead, but her suffering will come to an end now that my work is done. We will rise again the two of us, begin a new life."

"Yes, she will be rewarded in Heaven," the priest ventured. "And you will too, for the terrible cross you've had to bear."

"Have you heard of the phoenix?"

Fr. Scully did not reply in the hope that the man would give up and go away if he remained silent.

"It's a bird; it burns itself and then rises from the ashes. Renewal... a new life."

Fr. Scully went straight into the prayer of absolution. He was walking out right now, and he didn't care if the sinner wanted to stay all day in the confessional box, he was going and that was it.

"You may go now my, son," he said giving the man one more chance to finish up before he got up to leave himself.

There was no reaction, prompting the priest to peer through the metal grid. Much to his delight, it was empty.

Fr. Scully did not waste much time getting out of the church. After locking the big heavy door behind him, he moved as fast as he could for fear the confessor would reappear for another soul-searching session.

He was never so grateful to see his own front door as he was right now. He sighed with relief.

After making himself a mug of tea, he sank into his favourite armchair which occupied a place right in front of the Aga cooker that never stopped operating; even on the hottest of days it was on, because the house was so cold and damp it needed the backup.

The priest gratefully began sucking on his pipe and rewound what had just transpired in the confessional box.

What lunatic asylum had that young fellow escaped from? Killed three people indeed. Fr. Scully couldn't help smiling.

Within ten minutes he'd wound down, and after a second mug of tea and a nice dose of nicotine cruising through his veins, he began to think about the young man again.

Carefully he went over everything that had been said, because now he was not dismissing the story as the ranting of a raving lunatic.

There had been three murders in the town, he realized with horror, Judge Mangan, Sally Nolan, and Dr Curtin.

Fr. Scully sat bolt upright. Was it possible that the Magnerstown murderer had been confessing to him, and all he'd done was fob him off?

The fellow had said his mother was in a nursing home. That wasn't hard to figure out seeing there was only the one in the area, and yes, he did go to Mary I's every Sunday to say mass in the little chapel. Afterwards he'd bless the patients who were unable to attend. There was only the two: a man, and that poor lady who'd lost her speech. What was her name? He racked his brains. Mary Hammond, that was it, her name was written on a little card above her bed, and the confessor was her son. What should he do? Report it?

But he couldn't really get involved, because there was that little matter of the sacramental seal. When he decided he was going to become a man of the cloth, he had to study the code of Canon Law, eye-watering stuff it was too.

He was caught in a terrible dilemma, like the priest in that film he'd seen years ago. A fellow confessed he'd killed a man. A real nail-biting story now that he remembered the thread of it, which is exactly what you'd expect from an Alfred Hitchcock thriller. They didn't make them like that anymore and more's the pity. He sighed as he made his way into the parlour.

His film would be on in twenty minutes' time, and he was going to enjoy every bit of it. He would switch off from the world and transfer his whole attention to the drama, he'd savour every scene, and to hell with everything and everybody else.

In his heart and soul though, he knew he wouldn't be able to do that, because this murder confession business would keep niggling away at him, like a dripping tap in the background of his mind, drip... drip... drip. A dripping tap is like a nagging wife, his father used to say, but the difference between the two is that you can cure the tap, but not the wife.

"No," he told his reflection on the television screen, as he bent down to switch the set on. "You are not going to dwell on it, you've switched this on, now switch your head off."

Filled with a new determination, he made his way to the sofa. He was not going to let the whole sorry business get to him. Why should he have to do anything about the situation? Let the police catch the killer, it was their job after all and not his.

CHAPTER 46

Katie Manning stood in front of the full-length mirror and straightened her nurse's cap and apron.

She made a mental list of what she had to do, change the sheets in numbers four and five, but first she'd check in on Mrs Hammond. The poor woman had been uttering a few words in the last few days; granted, the words didn't make sense, but nevertheless her voice box was starting to work again. It would be wonderful if she got her speech back, Katie thought as she hurried to Mary's room.

"Hello, Mrs Hammond." Katie stopped abruptly at the sight of Greg standing by the bed.

"What are you doing here?" she asked. Noticing the gleam of the knife, an icy shiver went right through her body.

Greg waved the knife menacingly. "You are going to do as I say, or else," he said.

"What do you want?" Katie asked.

"Help me get her into this wheelchair, we are going on a trip, see? All three of us."

Katie did as she was told, her mind in turmoil. She was the only one on duty, because the other nurse had gone to lunch and wouldn't be back for at least another half an hour.

Pointing the knife to the exit that led to the backyard where he had parked his campervan, Greg said, "Right, push her out that way."

Once they reached the van, Greg knew he would have to gag and bind Katie's hands behind her back. He was taking no chances with this one; she was feisty enough to cause him grief. After he'd got his mother settled, he took off.

Katie's mind was working overtime. Mary Hammond's absence would be enough to set the ball rolling. James was right when he said that he didn't trust Greg Joubert. She was in a terrible dilemma, this fellow was dangerous and not one to be tackled, at least not by a little weakling like her. She saw the way he had lifted his mother, wheelchair and all with no effort in the least, and placed her in the van.

It seemed like no time at all before the van came to a halt. They'd reached their destination, Katie realized, but where was that? The windows of the van were blacked out so she had no clue at all where they were.

Katie focused on the walls of the van which were covered with photos and newspaper cuttings. The photos were of people who were clearly dead. All that blood and gore, what kind of monster was she dealing with here?

The hair stood up on the back of her neck because she knew exactly what the situation was, Greg Joubert was the Magnerstown murderer and it looked as though he hadn't finished with his grisly deeds yet.

Suddenly, the truth dawned on her. She would be the next victim to make the front page of *The Crier*.

Greg opened the gates of Green Park with the keys he'd procured from Toby Jackson. With a bit of luck, he would have finished what he came here to do before that Toby clown could escape and raise the alarm.

After carefully manoeuvring the van inside, he quickly locked the gates behind him and resumed his position behind the wheel.

"We're here, Ma," he announced as the big house came into view.

CHAPTER 47

When the troubled priest saw the young man standing on his doorstep, an expression of doubt appeared on his face.

James couldn't help wondering if the priest's lack of trust in him was because of his appearance. The long hair was more than likely the culprit, and his age wouldn't help either. People never put their faith in males with that deadly combination, hair and youth.

The priest beckoned James to follow him inside.

"My boss is not around at the moment, so I'm afraid you're stuck with me," James explained. He couldn't figure out where exactly Robert had disappeared to. He had not turned up at the station, and he was not at home when he called there.

Fr. Scully sighed resignedly with the thought that James looked more like an artist than a policeman as he led him into the parlour.

"So how can I help you, Father?" James had to raise his voice above the sound of the television.

Fr. Scully, taking the hint, turned the sound right down before facing James.

"I had a man here... well, not in here exactly," the priest said. "In the church... confession, you see."

"Oh right."

"I thought he couldn't be right in the head when he said he had committed three murders."

"Go on," James said.

"Well, I dismissed the idea immediately, it was just the ravings of a madman I thought, but having slept on it so to speak, without actually sleeping if you get my meaning…" The priest laughed nervously. "Anyway, I started to have doubts, so I said to hell with it, I'll call you people. It's better to be safe than sorry, isn't it?"

"It is, but do you know who this man is?" James asked.

Father Scully was glued to the television screen. There was a volcanic explosion in process and it looked spellbinding.

"Do you know who the man is?" James repeated the question.

Frank Sinatra had appeared onscreen and he seemed to be making his mind up on whether or not to go back to rescue the unfortunate Spencer Tracy.

"He's the son of that poor little lady in Mary Immaculate's," the priest answered.

James instantly knew who he was talking about. "Greg Joubert," he said softly.

"Is that his name, Joubert? Doesn't sound Irish."

"That's Spencer Tracy, isn't it?" James remarked.

"I didn't think you'd know one so old."

"It's called *The Devil at Four*," James said.

The priest grinned. "You're surely not a fan."

"No, but my mother is. She loves the old black-and-whites." James took out his mobile and hurriedly dialled Katie's number.

The prompt to leave a message kicked in. He rang again in case she hadn't heard it ringing. She didn't always keep it switched on when she was on duty.

"Still no joy," James announced as he dialled Mary I's main phone.

"Good afternoon," the voice at the other end said.

"Is Katie Manning there?" James asked.

"Who's speaking?"

"James Sayder."

"You're the police guy, we've just rang the station looking for you. I'm Mark, by the way, I met you in the pub, I was with Katie, remember?"

"What's wrong?" James felt panic rising up from the pit of his stomach.

"Katie's gone missing."

"What?"

"And Mary, Mrs Hammond, that is; she's gone missing too."

"For fuck sake." James ended the call abruptly. "Sorry, Father."

"Don't mention it." Fr. Scully smiled.

"They've gone missing," James said.

Fr. Scully nodded. "I know, I could hear. But listen to me now, there's more."

"Well?"

"This Joubert fellow was talking a load of gibberish. He was going on about renewal, and rising from the ashes."

"You did good contacting us, and you've been very helpful," James said, and then made a dash to the front door. He knew exactly where they'd gone.

"I've got to get the keys to the judge's place from the solicitors," James said as he opened the big, heavy door.

"You'll be lucky, they've closed down for the annual holidays, and Carter Jones always goes to his villa in Spain," Fr. Scully shouted out from the parlour, his spirits lifting as he congratulated himself for having done his duty.

It was true, he'd broken the confidence of confession, but nobody could fault him for that, it was a matter of life and death after all.

"Toby Jackson's got keys too," James shouted back before pulling the front door behind him with such force that the noise it made reverberated like a clap of thunder.

The whole town had gone mad, Fr. Scully couldn't help thinking. The superintendent confessing to infidelity, was it approval he was looking for? He'd got the young Polish woman who worked at his house into trouble. He was buying Cliff's apartment, he'd said, and they were both moving in, and he didn't give a damn what his wife Helen thought.

Changes were afoot in the town. The restaurant was being bought by the waiter Pieter. His family owned a chain of hotels back in Poland, and they were setting him up here.

Imagine sly old Cliff arranging all that from Spain. With a bit of luck he and Mr Carter Jones might meet up and discuss the consequences of actions.

Fr. Scully switched off at this point. There was three-quarters of an hour of the film left, so he'd be able to see the end of it, and that was good enough for him. He smiled as he turned the volume up and then eased himself into his usual position on the sofa in front of the television.

Frank Sinatra had just caught up with Spencer Tracy who was playing the part of a priest.

"The collar suits Spencer, and Old Blue Eyes really looks the part of the convict," Fr. Scully said aloud as he lit his pipe and thanked God for the simple things in life.

CHAPTER 48

Toby Jackson felt sick for the want of a cigarette. He had read somewhere that the withdrawal symptoms from nicotine made you feel a million times worse than the way you'd feel if you were coming off heroin, and that was a theory he could well agree with this very minute.

He'd never tried drugs, although he did admit to smoking a bit of cannabis once, and it did nothing for him, so there was no point in developing a taste for something that didn't work.

Toby resigned himself to the sad fact that there was no way he could free himself from this predicament, he'd spent the best part of an hour trying to disentangle himself and failed miserably. He'd just have to accept his inevitable untimely ending, and maybe with a bit of luck he mightn't suffer too much. What was that fellow doing with the keys to the judge's gaff? His mind began to wander. What was the fellow after? And that voice of his, the strange accent, it sounded so familiar. Obviously they'd met in the pub, or the bookies' maybe.

Like a bolt from the blue he remembered. It was the night before the judge was killed. Toby had been so drunk after all the free booze that he could hardly walk, but someone had come to his aid when he staggered outside the pub. That person had helped get him home, holding him steady when necessary along the way, and finally opening the door with the key lifted from its hiding place. That someone wasn't being a good citizen for nothing. So, that was how the stranger got the key to the courthouse, he'd helped himself to the bunch of keys that were always left on the kitchen table because Toby never brought them with him when he was going to the pub for fear of losing them. It was as clear as the nose on your face; the fellow dumped him on the bed and helped himself to what he'd come for – the key to the courthouse.

"Jesus Christ," Toby mumbled as the reality kicked in. "That fellow was the killer."

The unmistakable sound of a football making contact with the window surprised him momentarily. It couldn't be the young lad from across the road. Hadn't he gone shopping with his parents?

Craning his neck he was able to make out a little round red face pressed up against the window.

It was indeed the boy from across the road. Toby started shouting instructions, but all that came out was his Donald Duck impression.

When the boy disappeared, Toby felt his world collapse.

But the sound of the back door opening was like music to his ears, the stranger had done something right by unbolting the door and leaving that way – what a stroke of luck.

"What are you doing?" the boy asked.

Toby shifted in the chair, with a pained expression on his face.

The boy went to the dresser drawer and rooted amongst the cutlery for something to cut the ties off.

"I thought you'd gone off with your parents," the gagless Toby asked.

"I'm supposed to be sick in bed. You won't tell them, will you? I hate that shopping thing you see. My Mam spends hours looking for something to wear and then she goes back and buys the first thing she looked at."

"That's women for you," Toby laughed. "They're terrible at making their minds up."

"She'll kill me if she finds out I got up, and my Dad will go berserk because he hates me lying. I'll be grounded for a fortnight."

"Don't worry son, you won't be in trouble, in fact you're the hero of the hour."

"Am I?" the boy said incredulously.

"Yes, you're just like Batman's helper. What was his name?"

"Robin."

"Yes, that's the lad."

"I'm Robin," the boy said proudly.

"Now I have to report the man who did this to me, something's terribly wrong. He's going to do something awful, I can feel it in my water," Toby announced.

"Can I come too?"

"Course you can, you're a witness, aren't you?" Toby smiled.

The boy's eyes lit up at the thought of the impending adventure, and Toby couldn't help thinking he wasn't such a bad young lad after all.

CHAPTER 49

"That nun in Cape Town has laid claim to this place. She'll be getting it over my dead body," Greg snarled. "In fact, she'll be getting it over all our dead bodies."

Katie's mind was in turmoil. Even if she ran now and got away from this crazy man, how would she get out? He'd locked those big entrance gates, and anyway she was completely helpless with her hands tied. She was trapped like a wild animal with no chance of escape, and her stomach felt sick at the thought of how utterly useless she was in the situation. She was as helpless as Mary Hammond in that wheelchair of hers – totally and utterly incapable of doing anything constructive. She was certain of one thing though, by now the alarm would have been raised at Mary I's, but there'd be no way they'd know where to look.

"She'd just give the money she'd make on this place to the convent."

The hall stank of stale air and some other strong smell that Katie couldn't quite make out, except whatever it was had caused Mary Hammond to cough uncontrollably.

Greg looked concerned. "You alright, Ma?"

"How can you put her through this?" Katie shouted on discovering the gag had loosened on her mouth, she wanted to sound brave even though her heart was pounding in her chest.

Greg's reply was a slap across the face, and she reeled, completely taken unawares.

"Now keep your mouth shut," he ordered. "If you don't, I'll tie that gag back on you and make it so tight you'll swallow your tongue."

He used one hand to push his mother's wheelchair, and the other to drag Katie down the seemingly never-ending hall. Finally they reached a door leading into what appeared to be a kitchen.

Greg turned on the sink tap, and after letting it run for a minute, he half-filled a mug with water.

Mary Hammond drank almost all the liquid, making grateful sounds as she did so.

"Better now, Ma?" Greg asked.

Katie could see that Mary Hammond was not at all pleased; if anything, she looked cross, like a mother does when a child is naughty.

That other smell was more prominent now, and as realization dawned on Katie she had a tremendous feeling of foreboding, the smell was petrol – there was no mistaking it.

"What are you going to do?" she asked, not really wanting an answer, because for some reason she knew.

"I told you to shut up," Greg retorted and slapped her again, only this time it was harder and with more malice.

Mary Hammond shot him a terrible look.

Katie had always felt that Mary Hammond knew exactly what was going on around her, it was just that she couldn't communicate, that was all that was wrong with the poor woman, there was no brain damage at all, and now Katie was certain that her theory was correct.

"Have you heard of the phoenix?" Greg stared into Katie's eyes. "Course you have, you're not stupid, I don't have to tell you about it rising from the ashes do I? You know the story, don't you?"

"You don't believe in that rubbish surely," Katie gasped. "It's a fable, a fairy-tale."

Greg spat. "Do you believe in Heaven?"

Katie didn't answer.

"You and your cop-shop lover believe in fairy tales too. I thought you might."

"You're going to kill your own mother," Katie cried in disbelief.

Greg opened a drawer and took out a box of matches.

Katie froze.

"It's time, Mother, time for a new beginning." He smiled and left the room.

"He's going to burn us alive," Katie appealed to the woman in the wheelchair. "And there's not a thing we can do to stop him."

There was an unmistakable whooshing noise. Greg had started his deadly plan.

Mary Hammond turned her head towards the back door, prompting Katie to run to it, but to her horror it was locked.

"Ka... Ka," Mary managed to croak.

Katie stood looking at the woman in desperation.

Mary spluttered again, and then miraculously she got the word out. "Key," she said.

"Where?" Katie screeched.

Katie quickly realized that a box on the wall was the focus of Mary's attention.

"Is it in this?" Katie pushed her shoulder against the wooden box in the hope it would spring open.

It would be such a shame to be so near to escaping and then fall at the last hurdle, she agonized. She struggled with the one thing that was preventing her from getting the key, the piece of material that bound her hands together.

She focused on Mary Hammond who'd had a rotten life, and with a new determination Katie vowed she would not let the woman have an equally rotten end.

They say you gain the strength of ten men when you are faced with a life-threatening situation, and Katie was now about to find out how true it was. She felt one hand come loose, she was free and now the rest was up to her.

* * *

The flames had now taken hold, and Green Park, alias Renovatio, was burning itself like the legendary bird.

Gregory Cornelius Joubert rushed into the kitchen only to discover it empty, and as the air rushing from the open back door met the flames behind him, he turned into a ball of fire. The stark reality that there would be no renewal was about to descend upon him.

Outside, James Sayder was looking on in dismay at the sight before his eyes. Never in all his life had he seen anything like it. It was like the house was destroying itself.

"You can't go in there," Toby Jackson pulled James back. "You'd be roasted alive like a pig on a spit."

"Oh Katie, you're done for," James shouted.

Then he heard the cries. "James, James."

The sight of Katie and Mary Hammond in her wheelchair slowly making their way towards him was too much excitement to bear... and down he went like a ton of bricks.

He hadn't fainted since the day he made his first holy communion, and that wasn't because he was fasting as you had to do in those times before receiving the sacrament, but because he had been chosen to sing a hymn as the boys made their way up the aisle.

He had wanted to throw up, even though there was nothing in his stomach to discard; then he discovered to his horror that his mind had become a complete blank, and he couldn't remember the opening words of the hymn, so wound up had he been over the whole tumultuous ordeal.

The dig in the ribs from Brother Michael had improved his memory though.

Quietly he'd started off with, 'I'll do what you want me to do dear Lord, I'll be what you want me to be,' gaining strength as he went along in the knowledge that he knew every last word.

At end of the hymn, which seemed like a forty-line litany, he took the same route as the other boys had done to the altar.

The feeling of relief that the worst part was over was overwhelming as he held his hands out to receive the host the smiling priest was holding out to him. He remembered wondering if he'd turned into a feather, he felt so light, like he was floating above himself.

The cold marble kneeler meeting the side of his face felt so wonderful, like a beautiful cool comforting pillow.

Toby Jackson tapped his young companion on the shoulder, "This is a job for Batman and Robin," he said.

CHAPTER 50

"You alright?" James murmured softly.

"Yes," Katie replied sleepily.

They were lying on Katie's bed.

James nuzzled his face into Katie's back, she hadn't changed her clothes since they'd got back from Green Park and he could smell the combination of smoke and sweat. "I thought I'd lost you," he said.

"You were my knight in shining armour, you were," Katie gushed.

"Toby Jackson and that young neighbour were the real heroes of the hour. And you were the one who got away from that terrible fire, and you saved Mrs Hammond. You didn't leave her behind and save your own skin like someone else would do."

"I wouldn't have found the key to get out if not for her, she was a hero too," Katie replied.

"You can't get very far without a key." James laughed. "Thanks to Toby's fear of losing keys he had duplicated every key he possessed twice over."

"He probably has more keys than they have in Mountjoy Prison," Katie joked.

"If I lost you, life wouldn't be worth living," James said.

Katie turned to face him. They lay there for some minutes just looking at one another.

James started to say something but Katie placed her finger on his mouth.

"I have to say this now while I have the courage," Katie said. "I have loved you from the first moment I laid eyes on you, even though you were with Patricia, I didn't care, I was planning on wiping her eye."

She took her finger away and awaited James's reaction.

There was no need for anything to be said, it was time for him to show her how much he cared for her.

Afterwards they both drifted into sleep still in one another's arms. The sound of contented breathing wafted into the air until James's mobile ringtone emanating from the kitchen interrupted the peaceful scene.

Katie opened her eyes and looked at James. He was sleeping soundly, not even a clap of thunder would wake him. Gently she eased herself out of his arms and made her way out of the room.

"Hello," Katie whispered into the phone after removing it from James's jacket.

"Katie," Robert sounded surprised to hear her voice. "Is James around?"

"He's actually asleep, is it something important?" Katie asked.

"No, only I've been away, I took a few days break to be honest. Just ringing James to know if anything of note happened in my absence."

"You haven't been to the station?" Katie said.

"No, we came straight back here to Forge Cottage," Robert said.

"Right... well, you enjoy what's left of the weekend." Katie grinned. "And don't go out, not even for a pint of milk," she added.

"So, everything's quiet."

"Oh yes, everything's definitely quiet now." Katie laughed softly as she switched James's mobile off and tiptoed back to his warm body.

Robert encased Maggie in his arms. "I think my friend, James, has been a naughty boy while I've been away," he said.

"He hasn't been the only naughty one, has he?" Maggie laughed.

"No, and the weekend isn't over yet." Robert joined in the laughter.

CHAPTER 51

It took the Butler brothers three hours of hard graft to clear Number One Eaton's Grove of all its contents, and they were not sorry to be finished with it.

All that now remained to be done was to wait for Mr Carter Jones to appear with the cheque for their labour.

"That wasn't as easy as we thought it was going to be," Jimmy remarked, puffing on his cigar with relish. "My lungs are destroyed from the dust."

"Yeah but I'd imagine any kind of dust would be less harmful than the smoke from that yoke you're sucking on," his brother Dick replied.

"Those blinking carpets were a bastard to remove. What did they use when they were putting them down? I'd like to know."

"Probably superglue," Dick laughed.

"Oh Christ," Jimmy moaned.

"What's wrong?"

"I've just thought of something."

"Does it hurt?" Dick cajoled pointing to Jimmy's head.

"No, seriously, we forgot something extremely important."

"Extremely important." Dick mimicked a posh accent.

"The fucking attic, that's what," Jimmy wailed.

The two men made a mad dash back inside the house, almost colliding with one another in the process.

"I hope to fuck it's not packed to the ceiling up there," Jimmy groaned as he pulled down the attic ladder.

But much to their delight there wasn't a lot there, just a few boxes of toys, a rocking horse, and an ancient-looking wooden chest.

Dick pointed to the chest while rubbing his hands in glee. "Could be money in that."

"There's only one way to find out." Jimmy lifted the lid.

"Well," his brother enquired anxiously. "What's in it?"

"Photos, letters and more photos," Jimmy revealed as he rifled through the contents.

"What's that?" Dick asked as he managed to get in a position to look over his brother's shoulder.

"Some sort of document." Jimmy unfolded the object of his brother's interest. "It's only some sort of certificate."

"Aw shit, I thought it might be a bond or something."

"Nah, no such luck, it's just a birth certificate."

"Is it belonging to her, the one who got murdered here?

"Sally Nolan – wasn't that her name?"

"Yeah, that was the good lady's handle right enough."

"She won't be needing that now, will she? Seeing she's got her final one, the death certificate that is."

"You're a laugh a minute, you are."

"I know. I should be on the stage."

"You should, because the whole town's laughing at you."

"Ha ha! Very funny."

"Gregory Cornelius Nolan." Jimmy waved the certificate in the air. "That's who this belongs to."

"Her brother, was he?"

"No, her son, here look for yourself," Jimmy handed the certificate to his brother.

"Father unknown it says in this section," Dick related gravely.

"Is that a fact?"

"Wasn't she some stupid woman now, all the same? Not knowing who the father was?"

Jimmy wagged his finger. "No, that didn't necessarily mean she didn't know who he was."

"I know that, I was only pulling your leg, you idiot, joking you know."

"Well, you're never going to be a famous comedian, I might as well tell you." Jimmy smiled. "It's all in the delivery you see... all in the delivery."

If you enjoyed this book, please let others know by leaving a quick review on Amazon. Also, if you spot anything untoward in the paperback, get in touch. We strive for the best quality and appreciate reader feedback.

editor@thebookfolks.com

www.thebookfolks.com

Also by Anne Crosse

If you enjoyed this book, check out the other titles in the series:

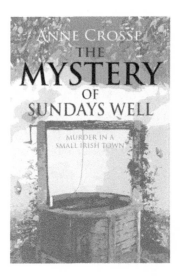

BOOK 2

When two bodies are discovered in a well, DI Robert Carroll is forced to return to the rural Irish backwater of Magnerstown, somewhere he really doesn't want to be. He immediately rubs the locals up the wrong way, and they are reluctant to help the murder investigation. Can the case be solved before his bad temper turns the whole town against him?

Available FREE with Kindle Unlimited and in paperback.

ANNE CROSSE

MEAT
IS
MURDER

CRIME FICTION WITH A DELICIOUS DASH
OF IRISH WIT

BOOK 3

A storm brews over the Irish village of Magnerstown when a recycling plant worker discovers human body parts. Detective Robert Carroll leads the investigation, but his focus is more on his next drink. Sidekick James Sayder takes the reins, and closes in on the culprits.

Available FREE with Kindle Unlimited and in paperback.

Made in the USA
Las Vegas, NV
22 February 2023

67970631R00132